We were silent for a long time, holding each other. Then Danny put his face against mine, like he wanted me to listen carefully once more. "I don't care about anything as much as I care about this band, Lisa. The other guys feel the same way. And if you're going to come on board, you have to feel that way too."

"I swear, I already do."

"I knew it," Danny whispered. "I knew the first time I saw you that you were like me." Then he kissed me, a long kiss. He held me and there were other kisses. Our kisses were promises; we would share the goal. We would protect our secret.

Margaret Willey

Facing the Music

LAUREL-LEAF BOOKS

Published by
Bantam Doubleday Dell Books for Young Readers
a division of
Bantam Doubleday Dell Publishing Group, Inc.
1540 Broadway
New York, New York 10036

ISBN: 0-440-22680-5

Reprinted by arrangement with Delacorte Press

Printed in the United States of America

June 1997

10 9 8 7 6 5 4 3 2 1

OPM

In memory of Judith Dunaway.

With thanks to Nathalie Ostroot, Wayne Snyder, and
Rosemary Willey.

CHAPTER 1

Dream House

$\mathscr{I}$'m stranded up here again. Every night since my brother decided to start a band with his friends, I'm either home alone or stuck with Dad, which might as well be alone. When I'm having my late-night cereal I hear Dad from the kitchen, mumbling questions at his computer screen in his office. The only question he ever asks me is *Need anything from the store?* Because when he heads to the grocery store, he stops first at his girlfriend's in the township and does whatever he does with her. He doesn't come home until after midnight. The girlfriend part is new. He comes back here, sneaking into the kitchen like he's scared of getting caught after curfew.

Yesterday I asked my brother, Mark, if he thinks Dad is feeling guilty about finally having a girlfriend.

"What are you talking about?" Mark asked, curl-

ing his upper lip as if I had just said something
insane. "Dad doesn't have a *girlfriend*."

"Mark, he goes over to Elaine Mitchell's house
every single night," I argued. "When you go over to
someone's house every night and stay for three hours,
something is probably going *on*."

"He *works* with her," Mark said. "They're both
accountants, duh." This is the way he talks to me
now. Like I'm stupid. He shook his head like con-
versing with me was such a waste of time, got up,
went into his room and made a phone call to somebody. Then he left the house without saying good-
bye. Rushing, like five more minutes alone with me
would have killed him. This is the way it is now.

But I didn't want to get depressed so I got out my
violin and tuned it up. I turned on my favorite radio
station and waited for this one new song that I love
to come on. I need to learn the words and work out
an accompaniment on my violin so that I can sing it
in my own way. The song has a refrain about letting
the deepest water wash over me and it's the most
perfect song for me to sing because I live close to the
deepest, bluest part of Lake Michigan in a house at
the top of a sand dune, overlooking the water. Music
saves me when I'm this alone.

Later that night there was a knock on the door of
my bedroom. Since Mark was gone I knew it was
Dad. He opened the door and stood in the doorway
in his winter coat, like he was afraid to come in.
"Need anything from the store?" he asked.

I asked back, "Why don't you just skip the store and go straight to her house?"

Dad blinked at me in surprise over the tops of his thick glasses. "Elaine Mitchell and I are finishing our annual reports, Lisa," he said nervously. "This is a very busy time of year for us."

"Why doesn't Elaine ever come here to work on the reports?"

"I don't have the right software," Dad said. He was getting fidgety now, frowning, squinting, taking off his glasses and wiping them.

I sighed. "I don't need anything from the store," I said. We already had about ten times more groceries in our house than we could possibly eat.

"I'll be home in a little while," he promised. "Don't forget to do your homework, Lisa. Mark can help you if you need it."

Like Mark still helped me with my homework. Like I would even lay eyes on Mark for the rest of the night. My dad likes to pretend Mark and I are still close, still making popcorn after dinner in the kitchen, still hanging out together in our pj's in front of the TV. I wanted to shout at him: *Haven't you noticed that Mark is never here?*

The question must have shown on my face because Dad put his hands in his coat pockets and gave me this look, this pleading look that means: *Please just let me leave.*

"See you later, Daddy," I said. After a few minutes I heard his car driving down the hill.

My song came on the radio right then, saving me. Letting the deepest water wash over me. I punched the Record button and got most of it, writing down the words so that I could learn them and pick out a harmony on my violin. That night I sang it a million times, alone on the deck, just my voice and the violin floating up over the dunes. Top of my lungs, really wailing; it's a good thing we don't have any neighbors. Oh, it's the most perfect, perfect song.

I've been thinking we should move, the three of us. I don't like being so far from everything. I've rehearsed bringing up the idea with Dad, some night when the time feels right and he's in the mood for serious listening. Because I know it will sound like such a drastic suggestion. This house was my mom's dream house—the house she always wanted—an old cottage in Highland Park with a view of the lake, decks on the other three sides overlooking ravines, completely private and quiet as a church on a weeknight. My mom did all the renovating herself, the remodeling, stripping the old tongue-and-groove siding, refinishing the original woodwork. She loved to repair things. Mark is good at this too—he repairs lamps and stereos and his car whenever it breaks down. He used to fix my bicycle about ten times a summer before he got so busy with his friends; now he's too busy to do anything for me. Now he leaves me stranded in the dream house.

My one and only girlfriend says she would kill to

live in a house like mine, so private and beautiful, like a bed-and-breakfast, no babies crawling on the furniture, nobody fighting over toys. "You're lucky you don't have to live in the nuthouse I live in," Patti Spinoza says.

I want to knock her off the deck when she says things like that to me. How can a person who still has a mother tell a person who doesn't that she's lucky? How can people be so blind? But I don't let Patti know how I feel. I don't want her to feel sorry for me. You can't keep a friend that way and right now she's the only friend I have. So I say something polite like *Yes, it's very nice up here.* I tell her that she can come over anytime she wants to. Anytime she needs a break from taking care of her little sisters and from being around her mother, who is not dead. *Come right over,* I say. It's not like I have to ask anyone's permission.

Lately I've started telling Patti more personal things, like about how mean Mark is to me now. She has one older brother who has already left home; she makes jokes about him, laughing at what a jerk he was. "It's the testosterone," she says, like it has nothing to do with her.

I wish I could laugh about Mark. "It's a good thing I have my diary from two years ago," I told her. "It proves that I once had a brother who was nice to me."

"He was *nice* to you?" she asked, like it was an amazing concept.

"Really nice. In my diary I have all these entries about him—Mark explained what thunder is, Mark helped me make a penguin out of papier-mâché, Mark fixed my bike and we went for a bike ride, et cetera, et cetera." I sighed. "Now he won't even talk to me."

"Look at the bright side," Patti said. "Another year tops and he'll move out."

Oh, that really makes me feel better, I thought. *Gee, maybe my dad will move out too.*

"I don't mean to sound like a know-it-all," Patti added. "But you really should lower your expectations."

I was trying to lower my expectations on the night when Mark's new friend heard me singing.

I was singing. Comforting myself by singing this bluesy Rolling Stones song about having a heart of stone and not letting anyone break it, never break, never break, never break this heart of stone. I had just finished washing my hair, which is getting really long. It's so thick that it's a big production to wash—it needs a ton of shampoo and conditioner. My mom used to help me do it in the kitchen sink. Now I do it myself over the tub with this long hose, which can be messy and requires several towels. I had taken off my flannel shirt so that I wouldn't get it wet and I had on only this white camisole with my jeans. I came waltzing out of the bathroom, combing through some leave-in conditioner, singing and heading for the living room to get my math book, and there, sitting on our living room sofa, was Mark's new friend, Danny Fabiano. He was smiling an apologetic smile, like he was sure I was going to die of embarrassment the moment I saw him and he was already sorry.

I stopped singing. "What are you doing here?" I asked, keeping my voice calm although I could feel my face burning.

"I'm Mark's friend, Danny," he said. "And I was just waiting for him—he's in the basement. I was just minding my own business up here, when I heard an *angel* singing."

"Very funny," I said. I turned away.

"Wait, I'm not kidding," he called behind me. "Hey, you forgot to tell me your name!"

I was veering back to my bedroom to die when Mark came up from the basement, carrying an extension cord and an old fan. His other friend, Ron Howader, was on the stairs behind him, craning his neck to get a good look at me in my underwear. Mark gave me this look—this vicious look, like I was the most disgusting sight he had ever laid eyes on. Like appearing in front of his friends in my underwear was something I had been planning for weeks.

"What the hell is your problem?" he snapped.

"I'm washing my hair, is that okay with you?" I snapped back. I pushed past him into my room and slammed the door. Then I went over to the mirror.

The underwear part was bad enough, but even worse was my hair—it was slicked to the sides of my head and dripping wet and my bangs were all corkscrewy and I looked just incredibly bad. And not only had Danny Fabiano seen me with my hair this way, in my underwear, but he'd also heard me singing at the top of my lungs. Worse, my own brother had treated me like a slut in front of his friends. I lay down on my bed and covered my face, wondering how I would ever find the strength to come out of my bedroom again.

The phone rang and it was Patti, thank God, so I told her everything. "You should have seen the way Mark looked at me," I said. "Like he wanted to kill me."

"What is *wrong* with him?" Patti wondered. "But get back to that other guy—what was his name? Did you say he was spying on you while you were washing your hair?"

"No, not spying—he was just here, waiting for Mark to come up from the basement, sitting on our living room couch. I thought I was alone. Patti, it was so embarrassing!"

She scoffed. "I can tell you a hundred things more embarrassing than that that happened to me with my brother. But I don't blame you for feeling bad if this creep was laughing at you."

"No, he wasn't exactly laughing. He was smiling at me, this little smile. He told me his name—it's Danny. He said I sang like an angel."

"Lisa!" Patti exclaimed. "That is a *compliment*!"

"No way," I argued softly. No one ever complimented me about anything, not even her.

"He was trying to say something nice to you!"

"He's Mark's new friend," I reminded her. "Why would he say something nice to me?"

"Hey, just because Mark hates you doesn't mean his friends will hate you. Why are you always such a pessimist, Lisa? Something really nice just happened to you and you didn't even notice it!"

"You didn't see the expression on my brother's face."

"Listen, can we change the subject? Because I was actually calling to invite myself over. This place is such a screaming nuthouse, I can't stand it another minute."

I could hear kids crying and yelling in the background. "Of course you can come here," I said, thrilled that she wanted to.

"Can I please have supper with you? My mom is making something horrible with eggplant."

"Sure, we have tons of food. Mostly TV dinners, but any kind you can imagine. My dad might come in later, but he won't care."

She was at my kitchen table in half an hour, asking me to repeat the details of what had happened with Mark's friend. She sat listening while I microwaved lasagna and frozen corn and muffins, recreating the whole incident. "You never mentioned that your brother's new friend was a musician!" she scolded. "What's he look like?"

I told her everything I could remember about him.

Tallish, dark hair to his shoulders, bushy eyebrows, intense eyes. When I mentioned his eyes, I remembered how they had been kind of searching. Full of questions. "Was he mocking me?" I wondered aloud.

"There you go again!" Patti cried. "Being the pessimist. Both of you Franklins—you're way too serious. I mean, Mark's not bad-looking, but all the girls I know are scared of him. He acts so completely unapproachable."

"He pretends that nothing bothers him," I said. "I think he hates me because too many things bother me."

Patti put down her fork and looked hard at me; she seemed to be gathering the nerve to say something. "Lisa, you have got to get over this thing about your brother," she said. "Can I be honest? It is making you extremely negative."

"I'm not negative," I insisted softly.

"No offense, Lisa," she said, "but people are starting to say you're kind of a downer."

"What people?"

Patti mentioned Amy and Karla—girls who didn't understand anything about me, girls who'd never had anything bad happen to them. I didn't give a damn what they thought. I said coldly, "Gee, I'd better hurry up and improve my personality for Amy and Karla."

Patti didn't catch the sarcasm. She went on earnestly, "This thing that happened today, for example. You could have described it as a positive experience, but you automatically described it as a negative one."

Could Patti be right? I cared what she thought. After she went home, I took a walk down to the water's edge, down a narrow, sandy path that was my private route to the beach. The sun was setting. I sat in the sand and closed my eyes and pictured the way Danny Fabiano had smiled at me. It helped to pretend that Danny wasn't Mark's friend at all. *"Where did you ever learn to sing like an angel?"* Danny asked.

This time I thanked him for the compliment. I just smiled mysteriously.

"Can you sing something else for me?"

"I'd love to," I said, *"but right now I'm on my way to a party."*

His smile was admiring. "Aren't you going to at least tell me your name?"

"It's Lisa," I told him. *"Lisa Louise. Did you say your car is right outside? Can you take me away from here?"*

Mark-man

Why was it my job to take care of her? I never said I would do it forever. I've done it long enough. Maybe I just got tired of Lisa expecting me to hang with her every night, answering her millions of questions, listening to her obsess about every little detail of her life, day after day. And no matter what I did for her, it was never enough. She was never happy. Never in a good mood.

Now she drives me crazy with her weird remarks about

Dad and the way she worries about how she looks and the way she always complains about not having any girlfriends and all that. I can't help her with that kind of stuff. I just can't accept it as my problem anymore.

I did it a long time. Years. Three years. Since the accident, I arranged my life around Lisa. Everybody expected me to— all the relatives and Dad, they all assumed that big brother Mark would take care of his little sister. I'd handle everything. I did. I saw to it that she made it through the funeral. I saw to it that she made it through the first month. The second month. The first summer. The first Christmas. The entire year. The entire next year. Mark can do it. Mark doesn't mind staying home. Mark doesn't need a life. Mark loves taking care of his sister. Mark loves helping her with her homework. Mark can walk her to school. Mark can keep track of her schedule. Make sure she gets enough sleep. Sit with her when she has a nightmare. Mark, Mark, Mark—I'm saying I did this without ever complaining. Thanks, Dad, for all your help. Feel free to jump in anytime.

Then last year I woke up and decided I just couldn't do it anymore.

I wanted my own life. I wanted a guy's life, with nobody dead in it and no little sister crying and waking up in the middle of the night and calling me and worrying about being alone and needing me to tell her when to breathe. I wanted freedom. I wanted to stop feeling bad. I'm almost nineteen—I just wanted to be a normal guy.

In the middle of senior year, I met this new friend, Danny Fabiano. He's a musician, he helped me get back into music because it turns out we like the same stuff—we both like blues and early Motown and Junior Walker and Buddy Guy and British blues from the sixties. We had so much in common. He let my oldest friend, Ron Howader, come in too. Then Danny decided that between the three of us we had enough talent to start a band. He seemed so sure. He brought it up like it was perfectly possible. Pretty soon we were all imagining it—even planning it. All through senior year we dreamed about the band we were gonna put together come summer, how we'd be in constant demand, playing at parties and street fairs and weddings and getting paid and basically having the time of our lives in the same town we were all so sick of that we could hardly stand it.

It was like Danny Fabiano gave me permission finally to have a fantasy again.

He told me to stop always seeing obstacles.

"But sometimes when I'm off by myself," I admitted, "I start thinking that the whole idea is completely crazy. I mean, look at us—who are we? We're not even real musicians!"

"You're looking at it all wrong, Mark-man!" Danny insisted. He was sitting on this old beat-up sofa in his private apartment above the garage at his parents' house, waving his arms, like some manic philosopher, explaining Basic Truths 101. "Look at all the necessary ingredients for success we already have! Number one, we have my old man's guilt money sitting in the bank, waiting for me to sign the checks. Number two, we have three dedicated guys with no complications to keep us from rehearsing every night once we get our equipment. Number three, we have a great practice space, right below us in the garage. And last but not least, I personally know at least ten girls who have massive parties every summer and would love to hire a live band, namely us. So we practically have gigs *already*. Look at the big picture, Mark-man! It's out there, waiting for us, believe it!"

"I believe it," Ron said. "And whose life sucks more than mine?"

Mine does, I thought, but I didn't say it. Ron's situation was lousy too. His new stepdad threatened to kick him out of the house at least once a day.

"Can't you just believe in this, Mark-man?" Danny asked.

"Can't you just wish upon a star?" Ron added, pretending to get all choked up. Danny threw a sofa cushion at him. Then we were all laughing and pounding the sofa and throwing punches at each other, pulled back into the fantasy. Danny could make me believe anything was possible. That was the greatest thing about him. That was what I needed most.

"I think I've come up with a name for the band," I announced. It seemed like the perfect moment to announce it.

"Nice timing," Danny said approvingly.

"Tell us, O Mark-man," Ron urged. "Give us a name."

"Crawl Space," I told them. "Because our music will be about crawling out of this hole of a life in Grand Haven. Crawling out through the mud and onto a stage. Finding something better. Crawl Space. What do you think? Is it good?"

A long silence. Then Danny said, "It's *really* good."

"It's too good for us," Ron agreed.

"You're a genius, Mark-man," Danny said. "I vote yes."

"Me too," Ron said. Then we all started laughing again, bumping into each other. I was proud of having thought up our name. So proud of the way Danny approved of all my ideas. He had already appointed me to be in charge of all band equipment, because once I had fixed his tape player and twice I had fixed the transmission in his van. "This is kind of a turning point, isn't it?" Ron asked. "We actually have a name for our band." His expression got really serious, almost scared. "I mean, what next, guys?"

"Next we buy you a new set of drums," Danny announced. "You can't be playing that pile of junk from your basement once we get serious."

"You're—you're *buying* me new drums!" Ron gasped. "We could be talking about a thousand dollars here, Danny."

"The money's in the bank," Danny insisted. "Courtesy of Vince. I have enough for whatever Mark needs too. Instruments, amps, whatever. Just decide what you need."

Danny called his father Vince, instead of Dad, and he was serious; there really was money in the bank for us to start a band. Vince's guilt money. But it made me nervous to think of Danny fronting everything. I was used to looking out for myself. "I don't need any money," I told him. "I've decided to sell my cello from junior high—I'm trading it in this weekend for an electric guitar. I found a really nice Fender—mint condition—over at the Music Tree."

"This is scaring me!" Ron exclaimed softly. "I mean, here we are, believing in ourselves enough to actually spend big bucks on instruments." He laughed his weird, crowing laugh, loving it.

"We're Crawl Space, starting today," Danny said, pointing to me, like I was responsible for the metamorphosis. "We're a musical entity now. We're a band!"

I pictured it then, sitting on the floor of Danny's apartment. I

pictured the guitar I would buy the next weekend, feeling it
already in my arms. I pictured us on a stage, performing. I
saw it coming. I felt how much it would change me. Nothing
sad about it—nothing missing, nothing broken, nothing to feel
except all this *excitement. Why not me?* I thought. Such a
long time since I had thought about my life that way. I said it
out loud. "Why not me?"

"Why not you, indeed, Mark-man," Danny agreed, toast-
ing me with a can of beer. "Why not any of us? Let's drink to
the band. Let's want what we want. Let's take what we take.
Let's crawl for it."

We crashed our beer cans together. That was the night we
became a band.

CHAPTER 2

The Studio

$\mathcal{M}$ark comes home even later than Dad now. The beer and cigarette fumes on him are so thick that I can smell him right through the walls when he walks past my room. A long time ago, when Grandma LeBlanc died of emphysema, my mom made us both promise that we'd never smoke, never ever, and I was right there in the room when Mark looked Mom in the eye and swore to her he never would. Then she put her arms around him and hugged him really, really hard and said, "You think it's always going to be easy to do the things I ask you to, don't you?" And Mark said, "I said I won't smoke, Mom. You don't have to worry about it."

Sometimes when I can't sleep, I remember little scenes like that and I wonder if Mark remembers. I wish I could ask him. But the truth is, we stopped talking about her after the accident, so I don't really know what he remembers or doesn't remember. I

don't really feel like I know him anymore. He comes
in all smoky and sweaty and stubbly from his band
practice; they practice every night. Sometimes I
overhear him talking on the phone about equipment
and chord sequences and how much this or that amp
costs and who's going to pay for what when.

I think it's a great idea, getting a band together,
not that anybody is asking for my opinion. I happen
to know that my brother is very musical. Mom used
to say he was a natural. He played the cello in junior
high and he was first chair. I remember hearing
Mom brag about it to her friends. That's why I
started the violin when I was eleven. The year before
she died. I knew how much she loved the violin and
I wanted to hear her brag like that about me someday. What did I know?

So the same week I met Danny Fabiano, Patti
and I were walking up the long gravel driveway to
my house, talking about the school day. Patti had
been especially nice to me all week—I think she
regretted telling me I was a downer and she was
trying to make up for it. We were halfway up the
hill when we saw Mark, Danny and Ron coming out
of my house; Mark was carrying a sheet of paneling
from our basement. The other guys were holding the
front door open, so that Mark could ease it through.

"Uh-oh," Patti said under her breath. "Don't look
now, it's the Three Stooges."

"Come up with me," I begged her.

She shook her head. "It's your shining moment."

She gave me a little push and then abandoned me. I had to walk the rest of the drive by myself, passing Mark and his friends as they lifted the sheet of paneling into the bed of Ron's truck. Mark ignored me; Ron gave me a half-wave; but Danny stepped away from the truck and smiled right at me, right into my eyes, like he especially wanted to see me up close again. "How's the singer?" he asked.

"Fine," I said. I hurried inside. From the picture window I watched the three of them crowd into Ron's truck and drive away. After ten minutes my phone rang. "Was that him?" Patti asked. "With the long hair?"

"That was him."

"Lisa, that guy was *seriously* checking you out. What else do you know about this guy?"

"I don't know anything about him," I admitted. "Except that he's Mark's friend. Oh, Patti, he couldn't possibly be interested in me."

"Leee-sa!" Patti scolded. "There you go again, being so negative! Have you looked at yourself in the mirror lately?"

When I hung up the phone, I went to my mirror and stared hard at myself, trying to imagine someone really liking what they saw when they looked at me.

People used to tell me all the time that I looked like my mother. They stopped saying that after the car crash, but I can tell from photographs that I look even more like her now, now that I'm taller and my hair has grown long. I smiled at myself in the mirror, trying to imagine Danny Fabiano smiling back

at me, that intimate smile, like he was seeing my
secrets and my secrets were okay with him. *Is it possible?* I wondered.

That night I tried to get Mark to tell me something about his band. I came up behind him while
he was sitting at the kitchen table eating a microwaved pepperoni sub, taking noisy, rushed bites. My
brother is a head taller than I am and considerably
bigger—big in the shoulders, with a thick neck and
a round face that's always red, like a football player's
after a grueling game. He has wiry strawberry-blond
hair—like Dad's before it started turning gray—and
coarse reddish eyebrows and hard blue eyes. My
mom used to say we two looked about as related as a
dog and a cat.

"What are you staring at?" he snapped when he
noticed I wasn't just passing through the kitchen.

"I was just wondering how things were going with
your band."

He looked away, scowling, and took another enormous bite.

"What kind of songs are you playing?" I asked.

He shrugged. "Older stuff. Nothing you would
know."

I kept my voice pleasant. "I like a lot of the music
you like."

"Trust me," he insisted. "You don't know these
songs."

"Give me an example."

Deep sigh. "We're doing mostly rhythm and

blues. Basically trying to find our own sound. We haven't quite found it."

This was a tremendous amount of information—almost a real conversation. I dared to ask another question. "Does your band have a name?"

He looked away again and pursed his lips tightly, like he didn't want the answer to escape from him into the room.

"No name yet?" I pressed.

"We have a name," he mumbled. "It's Crawl Space."

"Crawl Space? Really? That's kind of an odd name, isn't it? Why did you—"

"Did I say I care what you think?"

"I didn't say I don't like it."

"Did I say I *care*?"

"You don't have to be so mean about it."

"Would you just quit grilling me? I've got a lot on my mind right now. So go back in your little room and listen to your little pop station and play your little violin and just never mind about my band, okay?"

Something snapped in me. I wanted to say something just as cruel to him. "Who are you kidding, Mark?" I said. "You and your loser friends—you'll never be a real band."

Mark gazed at me for a moment, his hard blue eyes harder than usual. Then he pushed back his chair with a loud scrape, stood up slowly and strode out of the kitchen without another word. I heard him going down to the basement and I was sorry. I shouldn't have called him a loser. He wasn't a loser. I heard him angrily tromping around below me, starting up the washing machine, putting in a load of his own clothes. The three of us did our laundry separately; it was one more way we kept apart from each other. Hearing him down there brought a vivid flashback of Mom—I felt suddenly the way I used to feel when it was Mom in the basement. The person who would come up and ask me what was wrong and insist that Mark and I think more carefully about what we said to each other. *Mark, be more sensitive. Lisa, be more reasonable.* I felt her presence so strongly.

When Mark came clomping back up the stairs to the kitchen, he saw me still sitting at the table, one hand covering my heart. He set down the basket of clothes he was carrying and glared at me. "What is your problem now?" he barked.

"I don't have a problem," I said. "Nobody in this house has a problem." I went into my bedroom, turned the radio up loud and waited for him to leave.

*P*atti was supposed to come over; she was late. When the phone rang I was afraid she was calling to say she had changed her mind; I picked up the phone, ready to beg, but it wasn't Patti. "Lisa, *hey!*" a voice said. A guy's voice, pitched low and friendly. "When are you gonna sing for me again?"

My mind reeled. "Danny?"

"Good guess, Lisa."

"Mark's not home," I reported, flustered.

"I know, he just left practice over here. We have this great little studio at the back of my garage—you should come over and check it out sometime."

"Check it out?" I repeated.

"You'd be impressed. Although I must admit, rehearsal was a bust tonight. We have a long way to go before we'll sound like a respectable band."

I was thinking: *Why is he telling me this?*

"Lisa?"

"I'm still here."

"I'm actually worried about it, Lisa. I mean, we've got some decent songs we want to do and we're improving from all the practicing, but musically—I have to admit—it's just not coming together for us. Because something's missing, you know? Do you know how it feels when you want a deal to come together, but something is just . . . missing?"

I took a deep breath and admitted bluntly, "Danny, I just don't have any idea why you're talking to me like this."

He laughed. "Because I feel like it! Because I want to know when you're going to come over here and listen to us."

My head was spinning. Was he really inviting me? Just then there was a sound at the front door: Patti, rapping and making an impatient face in the square of glass. "I have to go," I said breathlessly. "My friend is here."

"Boyfriend?" Danny asked.

"No, no, it's Patti. Look, I have to go." I hung up and covered my face and rushed to let Patti in.

"What's the matter?" she asked. "Your face is all flushed!"

"That was him!" I told her. "That was Mark's friend Danny—he called me!"

"He called you!" she exclaimed. "Was I right? Was I right about him checking you out?"

"He was telling me about his band . . . like he wanted me to know all about it!"

"Trying to impress you," she explained knowingly. "Maybe we'd better ask around about him at school, find out what his reputation is. I'll ask some of the senior girls I know, okay? Just give me a week and I'll see what I can find out."

But Danny didn't give me a week—he called back the very next night. This time he sounded weary, even a little sad. Like he was trying to cheer himself up by calling me. "The guys just left," he said. "Another terrible practice."

My mind raced to find the right thing to say, something sympathetic. "Are you in a musical rut?" I asked.

His voice brightened. "That's it exactly! That is exactly our problem. We are in a true musical rut. I'm starting to think we need to move in a completely new direction. Like now, Lisa. I've actually been thinking about trying out a girl singer. And I happen to know that you, for instance, can really sing."

"Wait a minute," I gasped. "Are you saying that

. . . are you talking about having me . . . having me . . ."

"Having you sing with my band? I am seriously considering it, Lisa."

I nearly dropped the phone. "I couldn't do that!" I gasped.

"Why not? You have a terrific voice. It's expressive, it's loud, it's sexy. I've been hearing it in my head ever since that time I caught you washing your hair."

"No, no—that was a fluke, that was just me singing because I thought I was alone! I could never sing like that in public!"

"Why not? I think I know talent when I hear it. Why don't you come over here right now and sing a few of your favorite songs for me and we'll just talk about it. Nobody but me, no pressure, just a few songs and then we'll talk."

"Me come over there?" I repeated dazedly. "You mean . . . to your house?"

"To the *studio*."

"Now?"

"Now, later—whatever. I'm at your disposal, Lisa, I'm completely serious about this."

"Wait a minute," I said, suddenly remembering something enormously important. "Wait a minute, Danny. What about Mark?"

"What *about* him?"

"What would Mark think? About me singing in your band?"

Danny sighed. "I'll be blunt, Lisa. I know your brother pretty well. He wouldn't be too crazy about this idea at first. Which is why I thought it might be better for us to talk privately—make sure we're on the same wavelength—before we stick our necks out. This way, if you decide you don't want to do it, or if I decide it won't work, there won't be anything to explain to Mark. Understand what I'm saying?"

I told him I did, sure, sure. I was trying to sound like everything he was saying made sense, secretly feeling a kind of hysteria—my heart was pounding, my palms were sweating and it was taking all my self-control not to drop the phone and scream.

"So how about it, Lisa?" Danny asked.

"Okay," I agreed. "Okay, I'll try. Maybe I could come over now just for a minute."

"Fantastic!" he exclaimed. "Do you need a ride?"

I told him I'd ride my bike. I couldn't imagine being in a car with him. I couldn't imagine being alone in the same *room* with him, but here I was, getting the directions to his street, his house, his studio. He told me he'd be waiting for me outside the garage. I hung up the phone and realized I was shaking. *Is this happening?* I asked myself. I found my sweatshirt and my bicycle keys and my violin and I ran a hairbrush through my hair and was half out the door when Mark came barreling in, almost knocking me over.

He collapsed onto the living room sofa, holding his head. When he noticed I was getting ready to leave, he glared across the room at me and demanded, "Where do you think you're going?"

"Like you care," I muttered.

"Yeah, well, if Dad comes in, you're sunk."

"Tell him I went to bed, he never checks."

"I'm not waiting up, I'm too tired." He was rubbing his forehead like it hurt. He leaned back against the sofa cushions and groaned, "Man, I'm tired of having nothing ever work out for me."

It was so ironic. Because here was Mark who never admitted that anything was wrong, that anything bothered him, finally telling me that something in his life wasn't working out. He was opening a door to a real conversation, one where we might talk like equals about something real. How long had it been since that had happened? How many years? If it had only happened a week ago, I would have dropped whatever I was doing and sat at his feet and asked him to tell me all about it.

But that night I was the one in too much of a hurry. I was the one who pretended I hadn't heard. For once it was me, the little sister, running out on him.

I could see Danny from a block away, leaning against a light post outside a cedar-sided mansion, the garage behind him as big as a house. As I slowed my bike he dropped his cigarette, put it out with his leather boot and smiled at me, like he was proud of me, like he'd half-suspected I would lose my nerve. "Good girl," he called softly.

I got off my bike and walked it, coming closer. "Aren't you cold?" I asked him because I was cold from the ride over and because I couldn't think of anything else to say.

He ran his fingers through his hair; it was parted crookedly and falling into his eyes. He was staring at me through a few long strands over his pale forehead. "You won't be cold inside," he said.

He took my bike and waved me into the garage ahead of him. "The studio's in the back," he said. He pointed past two cars and a van to a small closed door, a door to a room that didn't look big enough to be anything but a closet. "You'll finally get to see what your brother's been up to all these months," he said.

It was a room, a tiny room, packed from end to end with equipment—guitars, amps, a shiny new drum set, a music stand, half a dozen mikes in pieces, two fans and a space heater. There were no windows. The room was still slightly smoky from practice and it held a mix of other odors that I recognized from Mark. Beer and sweat and a faintly metallic odor from all the electricity.

"Make yourself at home," Danny said. He went over to a tape player on a crate and fiddled with it a moment while I stood, awkward and uncertain, in the middle of the room. Scraps of paneling and carpet from our basement were tacked to the floors and the ceiling for soundproofing. There was a coffee can full of cigarette butts on the floor, a stack of pizza boxes, a pyramid of pop and beer cans along one

wall. The other walls were tacked with concert posters and band posters and music tearsheets. A desk-
sized calendar was taped to the back of the door.
Electric cords were everywhere; I was afraid I would
trip and bring the whole room down with me.
"What do you play?" I asked Danny.

"Bass," he said. "I'm lousy. Improving, though.
Just don't ask me to sing."

"Who sings?" I asked.

"Mostly Ron, which is a disaster—he can barely
handle the drumming. Your brother is a better
singer, but he refuses to sing leads. What d'you
think of the studio?"

It was like I had entered a secret world, alien and
chaotic and overflowing with male energy. It was
hard to imagine that I could ever have a place in it.
It was Mark's world, after all. "My brother will never
let me be in your band," I announced softly, suddenly sure.

"I think I could convince him, Lisa," Danny said.
"But first we have to decide for ourselves."

"It feels so strange," I admitted, "to be here. To be
away from home and *here*. In the place Mark escapes
to. Night after night, week after week. He's never
told me anything about the band."

"Not even what our band's name is?"

I nodded. "I asked him that. He told me it was
Crawl Space. What does it mean?"

"It's about trying to crawl out of our boring lives.
The sooner the better, don't you think?"

"Yes," I agreed. "The sooner the better."

"Relax, Lisa," Danny said softly. "Don't worry about a thing. Would you be more comfortable sitting down?"

"No, no—I'm fine," I said quickly. "I brought my violin. I'm pretty good, not first chair or anything, but pretty good. It's a really old instrument; it used to be my mother's."

I was still holding it tightly against my leg. Danny took the violin case out of my hand and set it down against the wall. "Skip the violin tonight," he said. "Just the voice. Look here." He flipped a light switch and a circle of light appeared around one mike. "Stand right there."

My throat felt dry. My heart was pounding. "I've actually never done this before."

"I know. Just stand tall behind the mike and start with something simple. Something easy to sing. How about that song you were singing that time I caught you washing your hair?"

He was standing close to me and he reached across the air between us and touched my hair with the back of his hand. "You have the most fantastic hair, did you know that?"

"Thank you," I said. "It's kind of hard to wash." *Such a stupid thing to say.*

Danny gave my shoulders a gentle push away from him, toward the mike. "Sing like being a singer in a band is something you want."

I closed my eyes tight and went over to the mike and repeated to myself, *something I want.*

And it came over me in a rush—the wanting of it,

the truth of what singing meant to me. How it was the only thing in my life that had kept me going. Suddenly it made perfect sense that singing would get me out, that it would be my escape. I would be in a band. And I wanted it to be Danny's band, if Danny wanted me. In that studio, standing at the microphone, it all seemed possible, that I might want something and get it just because I wanted it. My head cleared and a song came to me, a song my mother used to sing about a dusty boxcar on a southbound train. I knew it as well as I knew my own name. It was the song I had almost heard, earlier that week, coming from the basement like a memory. I opened my eyes, took a deep breath and faced Danny, looking at him the same way he'd looked at me, like I knew things about him. Because I felt like I did. I knew that he wanted to crawl out of his life as much as I wanted to crawl out of mine.

"I have a song," I said.

He was sitting on a step stool; he nodded and tipped his head to one side, waiting for me to begin. His face was hopeful; he was hoping that he hadn't been wrong about me. That I would be as good as he needed me to be. And at that moment, before a single note came out of my mouth, I knew that I was going to be good. I was going to sing better than I'd ever sung before in my life. I was going to blow him away.

"Ready, Lisa?" Danny asked.

And I was.

Mark-man

"Will you listen to me?" Danny cried, waving his hands at me. "I'm telling you, Mark-man, she is really *good.*"

I was yelling too. "You are nuts—you know that? She knows *zero* about music and she is only fifteen and she's my damn *sister!*"

"I know whose sister she is! The trouble with you is you can't see her any other way but as your sister! Hey, she's more than somebody's dumb little sister, pal. She has an incredible voice. I listened to her for two whole hours. I kept suggesting this type of song or that type of song and she nailed everything. She's versatile; she can sing blues, she can sing ballads and she can do the rock and roll too, if we ease her into it."

"This isn't what I want!"

"Listen to me. Will you listen to me? Admit how worthless the last few practices have been! Mark-man, I have this feeling about your sister, I think she might be exactly what we need to break out of this musical rut we're in!"

He went on and on for a few more minutes, but I had stopped listening—my head was roaring, I could've punched someone. "It's my band too!" I cried, interrupting him. "It's my band too and this is not the Partridge Family! I'm telling you, Danny, this is not going to work for me!"

Danny pulled his car to a stop at the curb and lowered his head against the steering wheel. He was drumming his fingers, grinding his jaw, preparing what he would say next. When he spoke his voice was almost a whisper. "I want you to go home," he said slowly. "And I want you to think about all the stuff I've done in the last month to make this band happen."

"Aw, come on, Danny—"

"No, I want you to go home and think about all the equipment I've paid for, all the secondhand stuff I've scouted out, how I totally cater to Ron's weirdness and all the driving around I do, day and night, for this band. Would you please just go home and think about that, Mark-man?"

"Look, you don't have to tell me this. This is not about me not appreciating what you've done for the band!"

"Then will you please explain to me why you are so sure that I would want something that was not in the interest of the entire band, including you? Would you please just explain that to me, Mark-man? Because I would be very interested to hear your explanation."

I had a sinking feeling then because I knew that he had already made up his mind about Lisa. Nothing I said was going to make any difference. That's the way Danny is—he makes decisions, he goes after what he wants. But this was my sister he was talking about now. And I'd already noticed the way he looked at her. Asking me why I'd never mentioned she was so cute. Asking me how old did I say she was when I had never said.

Danny turned his car into my driveway and pulled to a screeching stop. "Say something," he said. Demanding it.

"I just . . . I just wasn't ready for this," I told him. It was the only thing I could think of to say.

"I know that," he agreed. "Look, I know this is all pretty sudden. But I had a feeling about her and I didn't want to bring it up until I was sure. So just think about it, Mark-man.

Go home and think about it. Talk to Ron. Talk to Lisa. When you're ready to talk, call me. The three of us guys can sit down and talk it over. And I promise—we'll only do what's best for the band."

I grimaced when he said that. *Best for the band.* My band. The band he had given me. The band I had named. The band that was going to help me crawl out of my old life and start a new life. How could I possibly do that with Lisa tagging along behind me? She was part of what I needed to escape from. She was the sister I couldn't take care of anymore.

But I couldn't give up the band either! How could Danny be my best friend and not know what he was asking of me?

"Will you think about this and call me tomorrow?" he asked. He sounded impatient again, tired of my attitude.

"This won't work for me," I said, although Danny wasn't listening anymore. He was fiddling with the radio dial, finding his favorite station, tuning me out. I got out of his car at the bottom of my driveway and watched him drive away. *"This won't work for me,"* I groaned. *"I can't crawl out with Lisa."*

CHAPTER 3

*M*ark's Condition

"*S*omething's different about you today," Patti told me, her head tipped to one side with curiosity. "Something in your eyes. You look like you have a big, dark secret. Come on, tell me. What is it?"

So I told her about the audition.

"You did *what*?" she exclaimed. "You went *where*? Back up, Lisa! Danny Fabiano asked you to *sing* for him?"

"Sing in his band. Be the lead singer."

"Lisa, you never told me you wanted to sing in a band. I didn't even *know*, you never even *mentioned*—"

"He said I'm just what his band needs."

"Lisa, this is unbelievable! My best friend in a band! Lisa Franklin singing in a real band!"

On the way home, she pumped me for more details. "They have their own little studio where they practice and all sorts of expensive equipment. Danny

35

plans to be performing locally by the middle of the summer. With me."

"I can't believe you actually auditioned to be in a band. You are so brave! You must have nerves of steel."

"I was terrified," I admitted. "But Danny kept telling me that it's energizing to be scared. You just accept the energy. He is so smart, Patti. It's amazing how much he knows."

"How in the world did you ever get your mean brother to agree to it?"

"Mark doesn't know yet," I confessed.

Patti stopped in her tracks. "Excuse me," she said slowly. "Did I just hear you say that Mark doesn't know?"

"Danny's going to handle it," I told her.

"Hold it, hold it right there, let me get this straight." Patti was holding my arm as we walked on side by side. "Danny Fabiano auditioned you to sing in the band and your brother—also in the band—didn't even know this was *happening*?"

"Danny is positive that Mark will agree. Once he hears the tape we made of my singing."

But Patti had come to a complete stop again and was now making clucking noises with her tongue. "I don't know, Lisa. I just don't know about this."

"Danny will work it out," I said, growing impatient. *Have faith in me,* he had said last night, his arms around me.

Patti was still muttering, "I don't know." She was

walking again, shaking her head. "I don't think it's
such a great idea for you to get caught in the middle
of two guys. Didn't you say Mark and Danny were
close friends?"

She was trying to discourage me, and I didn't
want to be discouraged. I hadn't told her everything.
I'd told her about going to the studio and I'd told
her about the singing and about Danny's praise, but
I hadn't told her what it had meant to me, standing
alone in that circle of light, letting myself suddenly
want something so much that it was like a wave
washing over me, taking hold of my soul. I hadn't
told her that when I'd finished singing, Danny
hadn't moved or spoken for a long time. That we'd
stared at each other in the silence. That I'd held my
breath as Danny stood up. *I had this feeling about you,*
he'd said, *the minute I laid eyes on you.*

"Maybe you should find some other band to sing
in," Patti was saying, like I had a list I could choose
from. I didn't want to talk to her anymore. She
was trying to take last night away from me. She
didn't know how much it had changed me. Nobody
knew.

As we approached my house, we could see Mark's
car in the driveway; he was already home. There were
voices coming from the house, loud voices. Patti and
I looked at each other. "You could come over to my
place," Patti suggested.

I shook my head. "I'm not going to run away. I
want this too much. Mark has to understand."

As if on cue, we heard Mark shouting. Something incoherent, someone yelling back at him. Then Mark again, *"My band!"* The words came flying down the dune at me, and behind them came Mark himself, crashing open the front door, stomping down the deck stairs two at a time, racing to his car, slamming the door, gunning his engine. We watched him swerve out of the driveway past us to the road.

"Don't say I didn't warn you," Patti said. "Look, why don't you lie low for a while, have dinner with me and the rugrats?"

"If Danny's up there, I need to talk to him," I said, and I climbed the hill and went into the house alone. But I found only Ron Howader, leaning back in a patio chair on the narrow deck off the back of our house. His bony arms were crossed over his eyes. When I opened the sliding door to the deck, he sat up, saw it was me and lay back down again, rubbing his wispy colorless hair, his expression glum. "Ron, what happened?" I asked.

"Shoot-out at the O.K. Corral," he sighed.

I sat down in a deck chair beside him. "Danny told Mark?"

"Danny told Mark, all right. I got assigned to come over and try to reason with him. Which definitely did not work. He's freaked, Lisa. He's totally against this. He won't even discuss it with me."

"How do you feel about it?" I asked.

"Danny played the tape from last night for me this morning," Ron told me. He turned his face to me and a smile broke through. "I couldn't believe it was you, Lisa. No lie. I was truly impressed."

"Thank you, Ron," I said.

"But when I tried to tell Mark that I didn't think it was such a bad idea—especially with how pathetic our last few practices have been—he just *exploded.*" Another sigh. "He acted like I had stabbed him in the back. He says we're all trying to take *his* band away. But I would never do that, Lisa. I would never do that to Mark."

Ron looked almost ready to cry. He was Mark's oldest friend, one of the few people still in Mark's life who had known him before Mom's accident. "I know what this band means to Mark," Ron said from between clenched teeth. "It's all I have too. I sure don't have anything else going for me in this no-where town."

I closed my eyes, fighting tears myself. "Ron, why can't I have something too?"

"Before you came in just now, I was sitting here trying to figure out what Mark has against you lately. And I started wondering if maybe it had something to do with how Mark had to take care of you after . . . after what happened. Because I was remembering how after that, whenever I would call Mark and ask him if he could come over, he would always say he couldn't because of you. I mean like every single time I called him. I'm not blaming you, Lisa. I used to think that it was kind of strange, that it was like Mark's job to always stick around you. I was just wondering if maybe all that time of taking

care of you . . . maybe that's why now he acts
more like he . . . you know—"

"Can't stand me?" I interrupted sadly.

"Doesn't want you around," he finished. Then we
were both silent. Finally Ron stood up, running his
fingers through his stringy blond hair. "Look, I'd
better go," he said. "Maybe I'll find Mark, talk to
him some more, get him to see that he doesn't have
to take this negative attitude about you."

"Thanks, Ron," I said again. I was relieved he was
leaving; I wanted to be alone. I needed to think.
Mark had taken care of me in his way. That was true.
Was that what he thought having me in the band
would be like? A burden?

After Ron drove away, I wrapped my favorite
beaded black shawl around me and walked down to
the water's edge to think. It was late afternoon, earlier than I usually go down, and there were a lot of
people on the beach, strolling, walking their dogs,
flying kites with their kids in the May sun.

I passed several families having picnics at the
black wrought-iron tables that dotted the state park;
happy families, unloading plastic coolers, anticipat-
ing another summer. Usually it made me sad to see
families having picnics—sad and angry. But for
once, I didn't resent them. I saw those families as if
they were aliens—a different species, nothing like
me. I didn't want family dreams anymore, I didn't
want my dad to talk to me, I didn't want Mark to
take care of me. I wanted something completely different now. I would have to convince Mark that I

could change. The band already had changed my dreams.

When I came back up to the house, I decided what I needed most was to talk to Danny. I sat on the edge of my bed and rehearsed in the mirror what I would say to him. *Don't let my brother change your mind. He doesn't understand that everything can be different now.*

I dialed the only number in the directory under Fabiano and an older woman answered. When I asked for Danny, her voice became annoyed. "He has his own phone," she announced, like I was stupid not to know already. "Call his apartment."

"I don't have the number," I admitted.

She gave it to me abruptly and hung up. *He has his own apartment,* I thought, stunned. *His own phone. His own world.* I felt small and insignificant. I made myself call the number the woman had given to me, then listened to Danny's familiar, slightly sleepy voice on the answering machine:

"Fabiano here. Let's talk. Leave a message."

Just like that. So breezy and free. His own world. Could I ever have a place in it? *Have faith in me,* Danny had said last night. I clung to those words. I made myself believe that he would take care of it as he'd promised. He would handle Mark. I pictured him defending me to Mark, praising my singing, taking a stand. I imagined the moment when he would tell me that he had taken care of it, that it was settled, that I could have what I wanted. I allowed myself to fantasize. I made myself have faith.

* * *

"*Y*ou weren't sleeping, were you?" Danny asked when I answered his late-night phone call. He was whispering, his voice a rasp in my ear.

"No, I was up. I can't sleep. Why are you whispering?"

"I'm still downtown. I've been at the Kirby Grill. Listen, Ron and Mark just left. If Mark comes in while we're talking, don't let on that you're talking to me."

"Danny," I said. "Mark never asks me who I'm talking to on the phone, he doesn't care."

"Well, he'd care about this. We had it out tonight, the three of us, about the future of our band. And you and I need to talk about what we decided. Can we meet somewhere private?"

My heart was pounding. "Should I come there?"

"You're underage; you couldn't get in."

"Here?" I whispered.

"That isn't possible."

"Your place?"

"Even worse—the guys said they might drop in on me later."

"Could you come to the beach?"

"The beach—great idea. Tell me where to look for you."

"There's a clearing in the dunes between our house and the water. It's beautiful and it's private. You can park a little south of here in the parking lot and walk up the beach. I'll walk down and find you."

"Perfect, Lisa. I'll be there in ten minutes."

My heart turned over with joy.

*H*e was waiting for me, sitting cross-legged on a blanket he had taken from his car. He patted the blanket with one hand, inviting me to sit close to him. I did, but couldn't look at him. He took one of my hands and tugged it gently until I met his eyes. Then he put one hand on the side of my face and held it there firmly so that I couldn't look away. He said, "I have good news. But we have to talk. Because Mark has a condition, Lisa. A big condition for letting you into the band."

Danny took his hand from my face, lit a cigarette and took a weary drag. His dark eyebrows were knitted, shadowing his eyes. "We talked for hours," he continued. "Ron and I really lit into Mark for being such a jerk about you. And finally he admitted that it isn't just the idea of you joining the band that has him freaked. He's worried about you and me . . . about us getting together. Mark says if you come into the band we have to agree that there won't be anything going on between us."

My heart sank. "Did you agree?" I asked.

"What could I do, Lisa? I had to agree. It was absolutely the only way to get you in. And I need you both in the band. Not one or the other—both of you. This band is everything to me, Lisa. You have to understand that, that's the way it is with me."

This band is everything. Ron had said it too. "Are

you telling me that we can't be together, Danny?" I asked, hiding my fear behind a calm voice.

"We can't *appear* to be together," he corrected me.

I looked into his eyes, unsure of what he was saying, and he broke into a crooked smile. A challenging smile.

"I'm not sure what you mean," I said.

"I mean that we can only see each other in secret. Like this. And I'm saying that we have to agree. You have to tell me right here and now if you can handle a secret thing. You and me. For the sake of the band."

It hit me then that Danny was inviting me to be a secret girlfriend. Me, who had never been anyone's girlfriend. Me, who wasn't anybody's anything. It was more than I could have hoped for in a million years. I let his arm come back around me and I put my head against his chest, needing to hide my face, to hide how thrilled I was, thrilled and shaken at what was happening. "Yes," I whispered. "Yes, I can handle it."

He chuckled and held me tighter. "Then we have some serious practicing to do, Lisa. It's going to take a lot of work."

"I'm not afraid to work," I said fiercely.

"We're going to completely reinvent ourselves, starting tomorrow."

We were silent for a long time, holding each other. Then Danny put his face against mine, like he wanted me to listen carefully once more. "I don't care about anything as much as I care about this band, Lisa. The other guys feel the same way. And if you're going to come on board, you have to feel that way too."

"I swear, I already do."

"I knew it," Danny whispered. "I knew the first time I saw you that you were like me." Then he kissed me, a long kiss. He held me and there were other kisses. Our kisses were promises; we would share the goal. We would protect our secret.

When I came in after midnight, sandy and exhausted, Mark was looking for me. He came out of his bedroom as soon as I came through the door, blocking the hallway. I took a step back from him, covering my mouth with one hand, afraid that he would sense where I'd come from, who I'd been kissing.

"Where have you been?" he asked.

"On the beach," I said. "I needed to think."

"Are you too tired to talk?" he asked. "I know it's late, but I've been thinking too."

I followed him to the kitchen and sat down, watching his face, trying to read it. He didn't look angry; his skin had a kind of glow to it, the way mine looks after I've been crying, but that wasn't possible; Mark never cries. "Are you hungry?" he asked. "Want a bowl of cereal?"

I nodded, hiding my surprise that he was offering to do anything for me. He actually pulled the cereal box and two bowls from the cupboard, poured cereal for me and brought me a carton of milk from the fridge. Then he sat down, gesturing for me to use the milk first. "You don't have to do this for me," I said.

Mark shrugged sheepishly. Then he announced, in a rush, "Look, I heard all about the audition last night. The three of us—we've been talking about what it means. And we decided that we're going to let you sing with us on a trial basis."

Act surprised, I instructed myself. But it wasn't hard—I *was* surprised, surprised at how Mark was treating me. Trying to be kind. "Mark, you won't be sorry," I said.

"When Danny first told me about it, I was against it," he admitted. "For one thing, I couldn't figure out where he was coming from. Danny's a mover." He grimaced as he said it, embarrassed. "With girls."

"You don't have to worry about me, Mark," I said fervently. "I'm not a little kid who needs to be taken care of anymore. It doesn't ever have to be the way it was after Mom died."

Mark's expression changed; he looked like someone had flashed a too-bright light in his eyes. He leaned back in his chair, struggling with his response. At that moment, my dad came through the back door, a bag of groceries in one hand, his briefcase in the other. He looked at us and then at the kitchen clock and then back at us. "Mark? Lisa? Isn't it a little late for cereal?"

"Mark was helping me study," I lied. I didn't want him to interrupt our talk.

But Mark seemed to welcome the interruption.

"Dad, you probably should know that Lisa's going to start singing in our band on a trial basis."

"Won't that interfere with your schoolwork, Lisa?" Dad said.

"Dad, it's May," I said. "School is out in two weeks, I don't think it's going to be a problem."

Dad nodded. "I guess I shouldn't worry," he said to Mark. "Since you'll be right there to take care of your sister."

It was probably the worst thing Dad could have said. I glanced at Mark to see how he would react— he crossed his arms on the table and lowered his head. *Tell him,* I thought. *Tell him this isn't about you taking care of me.*

I felt angry at Dad for both of us, wandering in like that after midnight and saying something so useless. "Yes, Mark takes such excellent care of me," I said sarcastically, so that Mark would know I knew it was an inappropriate thing to say. But Mark didn't even look up.

Dad chuckled nervously in the silence, turned away, and began unloading cereal into the already brimming cupboards. I noticed that the back of his hair and the top of his collar were damp; he must have taken a shower at Elaine's. I pointed to Dad's back, trying to get Mark's attention, to point out this proof of Dad's other life, but Mark was lost. They were both shutting me out now, both finished talking with me.

It was proof of something I already knew—that we couldn't possibly have a real conversation about anything difficult, not without Mom. She'd been the one who kept us all talking and listening; she'd been our interpreter. She'd been the one who made it safe to feel things. No wonder we were all so lost without her. It made me want suddenly to bring her into the room in any possible way. So I broke through the silence. "Did you know that I can sing, Dad?" I asked abruptly.

Dad's back stiffened. "I believe I've heard you sing on a few occasions," he said guardedly.

"Remember how I used to sing right here in the kitchen with Mom?" I asked. My voice cracked when I said *Mom.*

The kitchen buzzed with a different, deeper silence. Mark's head was still lowered; he might have been asleep in his chair. Dad was standing very still, his back to me. Then he said, quietly, "Yes, Lisa, I remember that."

He was suddenly rearranging canned goods in a different cupboard, engrossed in it, like it was the most important thing he'd done all week. Mark got up without a sound, put our bowls and spoons into the dishwasher and left the room.

They're so much alike, I thought. On another night, in another mood, I might have gone to bed depressed about it. But on that night, I couldn't be depressed. I didn't care that they wouldn't talk to me. In twenty-four hours I'd gone from having nothing to look forward to, to having almost more excitement in my life than I could bear.

"You should get yourself to bed too, Lisa," Dad

said quietly, flattening paper bags to fit into a drawer. "It's a school night."

Like he cared that it was a school night. Like he worried about me getting enough sleep. "Whatever, Daddy," I said. *I have a new life now.* Before I left the kitchen, I kissed him on the cheek, surprising him. I felt generous. I was going to bed happy for the first time in years.

Mark-man

"She's good, isn't she?" Ron asked me. He was whispering, too tired to talk; we were both wasted from a killer five-hour practice. "I mean she is like *really* good. Isn't she? Isn't she, Mark-man?"

I couldn't disagree. Lisa's singing was amazing. I mean, you listen to a kid singing for ten years—singing around the house, singing to the radio, singing in the backseat of the car on the family vacations Mom used to arrange, and it's just a voice, a little-kid voice, something you mostly complain about because of the way it grates on your nerves when you're trying to concentrate or have a decent conversation or play your own music or whatever. And then there was that time of no singing, nobody singing anything, everybody just keeping quiet. And then you hear the same voice—that girl voice of long ago—feeding through a microphone, floating out of an amp, singing a blues song, and you realize that it's not a kid's voice anymore . . . it's a *woman's* voice. And it's coming out of your little sister! Those first few practices, I was in a state of shock from the first song to the last.

So Ron and I were driving home after this amazing practice—an especially long one. Danny had given Lisa five new songs to learn the weekend before and we had gone over each one like a million times. "My back is killing me," Ron groaned. "Is your back killing you?" He rolled his shoulders over the steering wheel, cracking his spine. "And I'm not kidding, I've lost all sensation in my arms. Man, how does your sister _do_ it? Keep singing and singing like that? She worked us into the ground tonight!"

"She did," I agreed wearily. My own fingers were numb and I had a pounding headache from too much caffeine. Ron stopped his truck at a stop sign and we watched Lisa fly past us on her bike, waving as she coasted down the hill that led to our driveway. She always rode her bike to and from practice, never once asked anybody for a ride.

"I couldn't pedal a bike right now if my life depended on it," Ron said. "That is one tough babe, my friend."

Being in our band had transformed her! At the studio, I kept watching her out of the corner of my eye, afraid of seeing signs that she was losing it and next she'd wimp out and start to cry or beg to go home. I waited for her to come to practice late, ask to leave early, bitch about how tired she was, how she didn't want to do this or that song over again. But she never once did any of those things. She was right there from day one, right in the middle of it, on time, ready to sing, always one hundred percent prepared. It made the rest of us work harder, too, to keep up with her. You couldn't be around that kind of dedication and not work harder.

"She's made us into a real band," Ron said. "Just like old Danny said she would."

"We were a band before Lisa," I reminded him. Ron had

a tendency to exaggerate. I didn't want to overreact—I wanted to stay realistic. Lisa was only our singer, after all—she didn't even play an instrument. And Danny was the one feeding songs to her, drilling her and making her focus on lyrics. She needed us as much as we needed her.

"D'you ever wonder how she can sing all these killer songs about having her heart broken when she's never even had a boyfriend?" Ron asked.

"We don't have girlfriends," I reminded him. "And we're doing the same songs." Sad but true—we were both hoping that our love lives would improve once we were a functioning band.

"She sings with so much *raw feeling*," Ron said. "Sometimes I can't believe it's Lisa."

We were silent the rest of the way up the hill to my garage. Lisa had locked her bike and gone inside; she was probably in bed. Before Lisa had joined the band, we used to go out after practice and hit the local hangouts with Danny, but now we were always too tired. As I was climbing out of the truck, Ron asked, "Think she'll be surprised about the brand-new mike, Mark-man?"

"Oh, she'll be surprised," I said. I was a little uneasy about the idea—buying Lisa special equipment, even though she was only singing with us on a trial basis. On the other hand, the mike she'd been using was a piece of junk—a secondhand, banged-up Shure. Danny kept insisting that she deserved something better and we agreed. When I mentioned that her birthday was coming up, that clinched it for him. "We'll give it to her as a birthday present," he said. "It'll come out of the guilt money, no sweat."

"Man, I can't wait to see her face," Ron said. "Won't she freak when she sees it? Hey, she won't get all emotional, will she?"

"I hope not," I said. But I didn't think he had to worry. Lisa hadn't acted weird or flaky about anything since she'd joined the band. It was like all her immature, overly emotional energy had evaporated. She was like one of the guys. My awful feeling that I couldn't make her happy, couldn't fix what was wrong, had gone away too. It was so much of an improvement that it kind of scared me. It made me feel like I wasn't sure who she was anymore. Which meant I wasn't so sure who I was anymore.

It was only June and she was in the band on a trial basis, but already nothing felt the same.

CHAPTER 4

Birthdays

"Can I please open my eyes?" I begged.

"Open up those big brown eyes, Lisa Louise," Danny said. And I saw, across from us, at the farthest end of the tiny studio, a microphone. A new microphone, gleaming and sleek and with a big red bow and a trail of curling ribbons around the stand.

"Oh, Danny!" I exclaimed softly. "Is it for me?"

Danny had put his guitar strap over his shoulder; he began playing the opening chords of the Beatles' birthday song, flashing me a knowing grin as he played.

"How did you know?" I cried. "I didn't tell anyone it was my birthday!"

"Mark told us," Danny confessed. "And I decided a decent mike was just the right present for our new singer. The guys agreed, of course."

"Mark told you it was my birthday?" I asked, amazed. I'd gotten so used to expecting nothing on

my birthday. That very morning Dad had tried to
talk to me about what I wanted, blinking and
clenching his jaw, wearing the expression he always
wears when he's scared of saying something that'll
upset me. "Is there anything special you'd like to do
for your birthday, kiddo?" He always calls me *kiddo*
when he's making a special effort to be a dad.

Oh no! I thought. "Daddy, I'm way too busy with
the band. We're practicing every single night!"

"It's just that I know that sixteen is kind of an
important birthday," he said. "I mean, there must be
something special that you want, isn't there?"

I thought hard, wanting to help him out and end
the discussion. "Maybe some new jeans," I said. I
couldn't think of anything else.

Dad nodded approvingly, like this was just the
sort of thing he'd been hoping I would request—
something easy, something that wouldn't require
anything from him. "There you go!" he agreed.
"Why don't you go to the mall with your girlfriends
and buy yourself some new jeans! Buy two pairs.
Any kind you want. Whatever looks good to
you."

He said this like it was the sort of thing I did
every weekend—shopped at the mall with dozens of
girlfriends. In fact, I hated shopping, never went to
the mall, and bought my jeans from mail-order cata-
logs.

Daddy slapped a fifty-dollar bill on the kitchen
table with a manly flourish. "Anything you desire!"
he said.

"Thank you, Daddy."

"Happy birthday, Lisa," he said. He put his hand on my shoulder and left it there a moment. I looked up at him and made an effort to look grateful. *Go to work, Daddy,* I was thinking. *There's nothing I want that you can give me.*

*N*ow, alone with Danny in the studio, I had just been given the birthday present of my dreams. A gift from my very own bandmates, a gift to show how much they believed in me. That they understood how hard I was trying. When I finally spoke, my voice trembled. "I don't think anyone's ever given me anything this amazing before."

"You were never in my band before," Danny said. "We can't have you using a second-rate mike when you're knocking 'em dead all over town. Turn it on, Lisa." He waved me toward the mike.

I turned it on and tapped the head softly, holding back tears. "I wish I could kiss you," I said, an amplified lament. Danny put a finger to his lips. Mark and Ron had pulled up outside; they were coming into the garage. They barged in happily, laughing about something, eager to start another practice session. They both stopped in the doorway, catching sight of me behind the new microphone.

"Isn't it beautiful?" I asked.

Ron looked at Danny. "You said you'd wait for us before you gave it to her," he accused, disappointed.

"Lisa was early," Danny said. "You guys were late."

"Thank you so much, all of you!" I exclaimed. "I can't believe you bought this especially for me."

"It's an EV!" Mark exclaimed softly, coming closer. "Jesus, Danny, you bought her an eight fifty-seven?"

"Hey, we agreed she deserves the best."

"Yeah, but an eight fifty-seven?"

Ron pretended to pout. "You never put a big red bow on my drum set!"

"It wasn't your birthday," Danny said. "Plus you don't sing as good as Lisa. *Plus,* Lisa's prettier."

"Danny, what did you *pay* for this?" Mark asked.

"Was it really expensive?" I asked, concerned because Mark seemed so shocked.

"Never mind," Danny insisted. "It's guilt money, meant to be spent."

"Why do you call it guilt money?" I asked Danny.

Danny rolled his eyes, like it was too long a story. Ron scoffed at my naïveté. "Haven't you ever wondered why Danny has an unlimited bank account for the band, Lisa? Where d'you think all this stuff comes from? It ain't from mowing lawns."

"I paid for my own guitar," Mark insisted.

"Yeah, but what good is *your* guitar without *Danny's* amp?" Ron countered. "Face it, folks, Fabiano *owns* us."

"I still don't understand why you call it guilt money," I said.

Danny explained patiently, "Vince—my dad—is basically paying me to stay out of trouble. He puts money in the bank for me and then he feels like a redeemed, responsible father."

"Ever notice how the Fabianos basically live in three separate apartments?" Ron asked.

"Not really," I admitted. I felt a pang of painful ignorance about Danny's life.

"The point is, Lisa, you deserve a decent mike," Danny said, ending the discussion. He came closer, stood behind me and reached over one shoulder, adjusting the mike head while Mark and Ron began tuning up their instruments. "Happy birthday, Lisa Louise," he whispered into my ear.

I was dizzy, breathing in the scent of him, feeling his rough shirtsleeve against my cheek. Then he whispered one more word: *After.*

The word I lived to hear. It meant that after practice, he would meet me at the water's edge. It was our secret sign.

"*Y*ou were so wonderful at practice tonight," Danny said. "Singing like a pro with your shiny new mike."

"I was overwhelmed," I said. "I'm still overwhelmed, Danny. It was probably the most incredible birthday surprise I've ever had." He wrapped his arms around me, pulling me against him. I could hear his heartbeat with one ear, the rhythm of the waves with the other. "I dread birthdays usually," I confessed.

"Yeah, birthdays suck, don't they?" Danny agreed.

"Your annual personal reminder that your family life is a joke."

"Tell me when your next birthday is so that I can do something as wonderful for you as what you did for me."

Danny laughed. "You're too late, Birthday Girl. Mine was in April. In the dog days before I discovered you."

"I missed it? Tell me what I missed, tell me how you spent your birthday."

He furrowed his brow, straining to remember. "Hmmm . . . let's see. We had one of our pre-Lisa rotten practices, I lost my temper at Ron, drank too much beer after practice, came home drunk and had a big fight with my mom about my phone bill."

"Danny, that's a terrible birthday!"

He shrugged. "I've had worse."

"Didn't they at least give you a present?"

"Oh sure, sure. My dad came through with a nice check. Appeased his guilt for another year and provided me with enough dough to buy a real birthday present for a certain beautiful girl who needed a microphone."

He hugged me again. But it made me sad to think of his having such a sorry excuse for a birthday. "When your birthday comes next year," I promised, "I'm going to give you a party."

He chuckled at this and cuffed my cheek. "That's very sweet of you, but I do quite enough partying already."

"No, I mean an old-fashioned birthday party.

With balloons and party favors and funny hats and a big cake with your name on it. Everybody singing 'Happy Birthday.' Everybody applauding while you cut the cake."

That made him smile and hold me closer. He asked softly, "Is that the kind of birthday party your mom used to throw for you?"

His question made the earth move. I felt, for a long moment, like we had both tumbled off its edge. No one ever asked me questions about what my mother used to do. No one.

He asked it again, "Is that the kind of birthday you had before?"

My breath caught in my throat, muffling my voice. "Yes. She loved birthdays," I managed to say.

"Then I'm really glad I made you happy today," he said. "I can't think of anybody who deserves it more." He kissed my cheek as I stared out at the water, overcome. Danny had asked me about my mother.

"Thank you," I whispered.

Then we sat in stillness for a long time. Until Danny broke the silence. "I'm ready to start looking for gigs for us, Lisa. I think it's time. I really do. Hearing the way you sang with the new mike tonight convinced me."

This brought my attention back to the band. "Sometimes when I try to imagine singing in front of an audience," I confessed, "I just can't believe I'll ever be brave enough, Danny. And I get scared that I'll disappoint you."

Danny touched my face. "You, disappoint me? Hey, who d'you think is watching you, keeping track of you every night, monitoring every note you sing?"

I smiled. "You are."

"Damn right I am. And if I thought you weren't ready, I would wait until you were. I would never rush you, Lisa, there's too much at stake for all of us. You have to trust me. Do you trust me?"

"I trust you."

"Good. You should. I'm an expert on the subject of you. And you are getting better and better every night."

I covered my face, overwhelmed at his praise. Danny put his arms around me again and we fell backward together until we were both lying side by side on his blanket under the stars. The moon on my birthday was the most perfect crescent—a silvery sliver. I lifted my arms into the night sky, laughing, my fingertips outstretched. *Even the moon is mine tonight,* I thought.

"Be quiet, Lisa," Danny whispered, pulling my arms back down. "What if Mark heard us?"

But I couldn't control my happiness. I was alone with Danny, in his arms on my birthday. I couldn't stop laughing with joy. Danny had to kiss me to make me stop.

CHAPTER 5

*H*angovers

*T*here was a scrawled message from Patti in the mailbox:

> You're never home. I've called every night for two weeks. What's happening with you? CALL ME!

I sighed as I folded the note into my jeans. There were so many things going on in my life now that I couldn't tell Patti about. I had been avoiding her since the school year ended. Still, getting a note from her gave me an urge to call her and explain how truly busy I was.

"I practice every single night," I told her. "And in the afternoons I have to learn the songs. I go through each one over and over with my violin. I never thought I could memorize so many lyrics in such a short time."

"Aren't you getting a little sick of it?" she asked.

"Never," I said. "I honestly love every minute of it."

"I can't believe I'm talking to the same person who used to complain about how lousy your brother and his friends were treating you!"

"It's different now," I said. "Everything is different, including things with Mark. The band even gave me a new microphone for my birthday, Patti. They all agreed that I deserved it."

A pause. "You never told me it was your birthday."

I didn't know how to respond. Patti wasn't getting it—she was missing the point.

"Are you getting along okay with that Danny Fabiano?" Patti asked, shifting gears. Her tone was doubtful.

"Yes," I said. I added carefully, "But there's nothing personal between us."

"Just as well. The word on him is that he gets around. Kind of a heartbreaker. Just thought you should know for future reference."

"Who told you that?" I wanted to know. "It wasn't Amy or Karla, was it? Patti, you *know* how negative they can be! They criticize people they don't even know! Danny Fabiano is a serious musician. I have a lot of respect for him. And my life has improved one hundred percent since he invited me into the band—I can't even begin to tell you!"

Another silence. "Well, I guess if everything in

your life is so perfect now," she said finally, "then you don't need me to keep calling you to see if you're still alive."

"I didn't mean it like that, Patti," I insisted. "I never said my life is perfect! I want to stay in touch with you. But I love being in this band. And I can't possibly miss a practice now. Danny wants us ready to perform by July and that's only two weeks away!"

Patti sighed. "So are you saying you'll have more free time to do stuff in July?" she asked.

I hesitated, thinking ahead, trying to imagine a time in the future when Crawl Space wouldn't need to be practicing every night. Trying to foresee an end to the intense, secluded sessions in Danny's studio, the center of my life now. It wasn't possible to imagine.

But I remembered something else. I remembered that Patti had been my only friend at school, back in the days when no one else seemed aware of my existence. So I promised her that yes, I would have more time to spend with her in July. And I told her that when the band started playing at parties, I would get her invited to all the really good ones.

Which made her ecstatic. "I would be so totally, eternally grateful if you could do that!" she said. "You cannot *believe* how boring my summer has been so far! All I do is make bottles, rewind Winnie-the-Pooh videos and change diapers. I'm going crazy!"

"I'll rescue you soon," I promised.

As I was hanging up, Mark's gruff voice startled

me. He had come into the kitchen without a sound; he was listening, his eyes narrowed in disapproval. "Who was that on the phone?" he asked.

"My friend Patti," I said. "She just called to see how everything was going."

"What were you saying to her about going to parties?"

"I just told her once we started playing at parties, she could come with me to some. So I'll have a girlfriend to hang out with."

"Who says you're gonna hang out at these parties?"

"What am I supposed to do?" I asked. "Wait for you guys in the car after we play?"

Mark scowled. He dragged himself to the kitchen table and sat down, holding the sides of his head. "Just drop the subject of parties, okay?"

I looked at him more closely and realized that he was exhibiting the classic signs of a hangover—rubbing his head, squinting his bloodshot eyes, flinching at noises. "Where did you guys go after practice last night?" I asked.

"Big graduation bash in Muskegon," he groaned. "Danny convinced us it would be just the right scene for finding somebody to hire us for our first gig."

"So what happened?"

"Something's in the works. He met some girl and now he says he's sure he can talk her into letting us play."

"Some girl?" I repeated. Patti's remarks about

Danny came back to me, troubling me. Mark was rubbing his forehead, grimacing. I knew it was risky to press him for information in his condition, but I couldn't stop myself. "Tell me about the party," I begged.

Mark poured himself a cup of coffee and looked back at me, focusing his eyes with an effort. "There was such a terrible band at this party, Lisa," he rasped. "Really lame. We are one hundred times better than that band already. And they were getting *paid.*"

"Was Danny having fun at this party?"

"Danny? Danny *always* has fun at parties," Mark replied enviously. "Every place we go, he knows half the people there. Look, why are you asking me all these questions?"

"I need to know . . . what to expect when we're out . . . performing," I said vaguely. "What were you saying about Danny knowing everybody?"

Mark rubbed his temples, thinking. "Although lately, I'd have to admit that Danny's changed. Since the summer started, he's changed."

"In what way?" I pressed.

"He isn't looking at girls the same way. He's more settled down and focused. Really putting the band first."

More settled down, I repeated to myself. *Because of me.*

Mark was grimacing, like even this much talking had aggravated his headache. He looked up at me, his expression disapproving again. "Look, none of this stuff about Danny and parties has anything to do with you," he grumbled.

Oh but it does, I argued silently. And I wondered if he ever would know. If there would come a time when I could happily tell him what was happening between me and his new best friend. Mark caught me staring questioningly at him. "Would you just *go away*?" he barked.

I did; I left the room. I knew he would be better by tonight, the new Mark, my bandmate, not my brother. I was actually feeling grateful to him in spite of his rudeness—he had given me a reason to believe that I had changed Danny's life as much as Danny had changed mine.

But now all I wanted in the world was to see him —to see the Danny I had changed, the Danny who was more settled down and focused because of me. It was hours and hours until the next practice—I couldn't wait. Even though it was still morning, I had to see him.

I knew the entrance to his apartment was at the back of the garage, although I had never been up there. I parked my bike in the Fabiano garage and went through, past the studio, to the back entrance. But once outside, I nearly collided with a heavy, scowling woman. Her hair was dyed a harsh black, her face was puffy and unfriendly. I couldn't believe this was handsome Danny's mother, but who else could it be? "Mrs. Fabiano?" I asked uncertainly.

"What's your hurry?" she asked, her voice congested, thick with sarcasm. "He's not even up yet."

I didn't know what to say. "I—I just needed to talk to him about something," I stammered. "I'm Lisa . . . I'm in his band."

She shrugged, like this meant nothing to her. "That's a new one," she muttered.

She brushed past me and disappeared into the garage, entering the house that way. I hesitated, leaning against the outside back wall of the garage, disoriented now, less sure that it was okay to be there. But I couldn't turn back. I moved closer to the door of Danny's apartment and knocked hard. The door was unlatched; it opened slightly under my hand, leading to a stairwell. I called Danny's name.

His voice came floating down the stairs. "Lisa?" he called softly. "Lisa, is that you?"

"It's me!" I called up to him.

He came bounding down the stairs in his pajama bottoms, pulled me by the hand back up to his apartment. "Did anyone see you?" he asked worriedly.

"Your mom. We bumped into each other. She wasn't very friendly."

"She's never friendly when she's hung over. Pissed off at me about something or other. I pretended to be asleep so I wouldn't have to deal with her. What are you doing here—is anything wrong?"

I shook my head. "I just . . . I needed to see you. Is that okay?"

He wrapped his arms around me and buried his

face in my hair. "Don't make a habit of it," he said, but he was unmistakably glad to see me. "Sit down, I'll get dressed. I have something to tell you. Pour yourself a cup of coffee, I'll be right back."

Then I was with him, sitting across the table from him, sharing coffee. "Are you ready for some great news?" he asked. "We have a gig, Lisa Louise. Not this weekend, but the next one—a *serious* party. In a huge cottage on the north shore—I was there last night. This place has a massive screened-in deck overlooking the lake—a fantastic place for a party."

"You were there?" I asked.

He nodded. "The girl who's hiring us showed me the space we'd be playing in."

I accused quietly, "Mark said you met a girl."

He made an impatient face. "I didn't *meet* her. She was somebody I already knew. She always has a big summer party at her parents' cottage so I talked the band up and told her we were ready to perform and it worked!"

"You went to her cottage?"

"Lisa, this is *business*. Aren't you excited about what I'm telling you? Isn't this exactly what we've all been waiting for?"

I nodded, letting it sink in. Our first gig. I put my coffee mug down, covered my face and confessed, "Danny, I'm scared."

"Hey, none of that, remember? Remember our talk about me knowing when you're ready?"

"But it's so soon! I'm still getting used to singing in front of *you*!"

Danny pulled my hands away from my face. "How can I convince you?" he asked.

I saw my moment and I asked: "Spend today with me?"

Danny let go of my hands. "Lisa, you know that's impossible."

"Just one day, Danny. One day of being with you. It will make me brave, I know it will and no one will know."

He thought about it, softening. "We could go up north," he said, thinking aloud. He asked, "Did you ride your bike?"

I nodded. "It's outside."

"We'll hide it in the back of the van and drive out of town while it's still early. Just you and me. Is that what you want, Lisa?"

"Yes," I said.

He opened his arms. "Take me away from these little-town blues," he sang. He had a scratchy off-key voice; it made me laugh whenever I heard it. We were both laughing; we laughed all the way down to the van, laughed while we put my bike into the back, laughed as we drove out of town. Danny made me crouch in the front of the van until we were a few miles away, which seemed absurd and made us laugh harder, hysterically, like little kids getting away with something.

It was the most gorgeous, blue-sky June morning. I had never been alone with Danny in daylight before. I realized, sitting beside him as he drove, how much I had been needing exactly this—to feel like we were a normal couple out in the normal world. But if we were going to feel like a couple, it seemed to me that we needed to know more about each other. And so I asked him, hoping that he wouldn't mind, "Is your mom like that a lot, Danny? The way she was today?"

He was fiddling with the radio knobs in his car, trying to find a song he liked. "You mean hung over?" he asked. "She's an alcoholic, Lisa. Don't be shocked, I'm used to it."

"It doesn't seem like the sort of thing a person would get used to."

"Wrong, Lisa. People can get used to anything. You of all people should know."

"Why should I know?"

"Because of what happened to your mom."

My heart seemed to stop beating. He had done it again. He had mentioned the thing no one ever mentioned, the person no one ever named. After a moment of silence, I asked softly, "Who told you what happened to my mom?"

"It wasn't Mark," Danny said. "Mark's pretty clear about not wanting to discuss it. But I was curious so I asked Ron. Ron told me about the accident. Was it right here in town?"

I nodded. "She was coming back from grocery shopping. A guy driving a truck fell asleep and ran into her while she was turning off Beacon. She never came home. The last thing she did before she left our house was to tell Mark that she was leaving him in charge of me. She was always telling him that, whenever she went anywhere."

"Explains a lot, doesn't it?" Danny sighed.

We were both silent for a moment. I rolled down the window I'd been staring out of and took a few deep breaths, feeling suddenly winded. Danny touched my hand. I thought he was going to say something comforting, but he said, his voice pleading, "Don't ever tell Mark about us, Lisa."

"I won't," I promised. He lifted my hand to his lips and kissed it. "I won't ever get used to what happened to my mom, Danny," I insisted.

Danny nodded. "I guess I was thinking more of Mark."

"Just because Mark pretends he's used to what happened doesn't mean he is."

The words came out of me bitterly. Yet I was feeling a kind of exhilaration. I had never told anyone the things I was telling Danny. The way he was listening was helping me, washing something away. He wasn't turning away from me, shutting me out, changing the subject. He was there listening, nodding and listening.

"People have to live in the present," he said, like he had thought about this a long time. "You can't change the past—today is all you get. You have to learn not to care about things in the past, not to dwell on them. Mark understands that. He never loses his cool. He does whatever it takes to just keep moving."

He was talking like he and Mark had this quality
in common—an agreement not to care. But I was
shaking my head. I couldn't accept what he was saying—that a person could decide not to care, not to
feel—especially coming from him, the person who
had given me a way finally to express all the things I
cared about. He was the first person who had listened
to me talking about my mother without turning
away. It was like gaining something and losing it at
the same time.

I stole a sideways glance at him; his mouth was a
line. He looked determined, like it was crucial to
him that I accept what he was saying. An old ache
came into my chest and I was suddenly cold all over,
shivering. I rolled up the window and leaned into
Danny, taking his free hand back from the seat between us; it was warm and familiar and I needed to
touch him. I needed to feel that nothing in the world
mattered as much as how we felt about each other.
He squeezed my hand, then gently cupped the back
of my head, stroking my hair. "Does that make me
an unfeeling creep?" he wondered aloud.

"You care about things. I know you do."

"I care about the band, Lisa."

"Don't you care about me?"

"Of course I care about you. You saved my band.
I'm so glad I found you when I did. Remember that
day I heard you singing at your house? You were
washing your hair? And you came out of the bathroom looking so pretty, and you were so pissed off

that I'd overheard you? You wouldn't even stick
around and talk to me. Remember that?"

"I was so embarrassed," I said. "You said I sang
like an angel and I thought you were being sarcastic."

"Turns out you *were* an angel. What a lucky day
that was for me. For both of us."

The coldness in my chest faded with those words.
The day was unfolding ahead of us, our beautiful,
stolen day. I had waited so long for it. Worked so
hard for it. *An angel,* Danny had called me. It was all
I wanted to be, for him.

When I was back in the house alone, late in the
afternoon, I had a strong sense of my mother being
with me. I think it was because I had talked about
her so openly. And because I'd talked about Mark
too, I remembered a photograph I hadn't thought
about in a long time. Mark used to keep it in his
room, in the top drawer of the dresser beside his bed.
I had an uncontrollable need to see if he still had it,
if it was still there. Despite the fact that we have this
unspoken rule about privacy, I went into Mark's
room and opened his top desk drawer, the place
where I had last seen the photograph—years ago,
back in the days when Mark didn't care if I came
into his room or not. Back in the days after the
accident, when he took care of me.

There weren't baseball cards or car magazines or
cuff links in that top drawer anymore. Instead there

were fanzines and phone numbers of live-music bars, a few girls' phone numbers and some Polaroids of the early days of Crawl Space, before me. I moved my hand under these things until my fingers touched something thick and heavy, the sharply curled edges of a studio portrait.

It was Mom. Louise Franklin with little Mark. She is wearing a long hippie-style dress, black with tiny flowers, laced up the front, and around her shoulders is the beaded shawl, my favorite shawl, the one I wear. Her hair is loose and wild, her smile mysterious. Mom looks like a gypsy. Mark is standing in front of Mom, wearing a little boy's three-piece suit. Her miniature man. The same Mark who is now so broad-shouldered and burly that he scares people away. The same Mark who has convinced his best friend that nothing bothers him, nothing will ever take him by surprise again.

Mark misses her as much as I do, I thought. I knew my brother in a deeper way than Danny did. I knew why he pretended not to care. I understood. I put the photo back at the bottom of the drawer, went back to my own room and lay on my bed. Mom was in my thoughts. I remembered how much she'd loved car trips. She'd always said we needed them, especially Dad; she'd say that he'd probably turn into a piece of office furniture if she didn't get him out on the road once in a while. She would have understood what today's trip with Danny had meant to me. I felt calm, lying there thinking about her in the afterglow of that beautiful stolen day. I was sure that wherever she was, she was happy for me.

Mark-man

"Were you watching her?" I asked Ron. "Did you notice how she acted when Danny announced about the gig? Almost like she already knew about it?"

"How could she know about it?" Ron asked practically. "Come on, Mark. Lighten up."

"She doesn't seem very nervous—wouldn't you think she'd be really nervous? She wasn't acting nervous tonight at all."

"I'm nervous enough for all of us," Ron said. "God, we are talking about a *public performance*! In less than two weeks! Did you notice how bad I was screwing up tonight? Do you think Danny noticed?"

"He's too busy deciding every little detail of what Lisa should do," I grumbled.

I waited for Ron to express amazement because I was complaining about Danny, but he didn't. I looked at him. He looked at me. "The thing is," he said, "she *is* really good."

"Yeah, yeah, she's good."

"She can sing anything, Mark. So what are you complaining about? And why are we both acting worried?"

"Why *are* we both acting worried?"

"If you tell me what you're most worried about, I'll tell you what I'm most worried about."

So I went first. "What if when we're playing at parties, guys start seriously coming on to Lisa? You know, because she's a chick in a band and everything?"

Ron rolled his eyes. "Mark, we are talking about Lisa here. She's not the type that guys come on to."

"Yeah, but you know how pushy guys are when they're at parties and they're desperate."

"You mean like we always are?" he asked. He laughed his annoying laugh.

I didn't laugh with him. "Okay, so what are you worried about?" I asked. His face got serious again. "Promise you won't say anything to Danny?" he begged.

"This conversation stays in the car."

"It just seems to me," Ron said, "that when all of this started, we were going to be a rock-and-roll band, remember? A garage-rock band? Remember how we talked about how we were gonna rock this town and everything and get as low down as we could get? Play the grungiest blues we could get our hands on? Remember that, Mark-man?"

"Yeah, yeah, I remember."

"But that isn't the direction we're going in anymore, is it?"

I sighed. "Not really."

"Sometimes I get afraid we'll lose that energy we started with and we won't be the kind of band I want to be in anymore. Does that mean I have a really bad attitude? Am I being a jerk? With how hard Lisa is working and everything?"

"I don't know," I said. "Maybe we should talk to Danny about it."

"Not now," Ron said. "The timing is all wrong. We're too close to the first gig. We'd better just see what happens. Maybe it will be so great at this party that I won't feel this way anymore."

"Maybe."

"Look, don't tell him I was complaining about the songs," Ron begged. He never complained; it was extremely unusual. Danny would have been surprised. But Ron was right about it being too close to the gig; we'd been working like dogs to get ready. I told him he didn't have to worry.

"Don't mention that I was worrying about Lisa," I said, and he told me I didn't have to worry about that either. But I knew we'd both probably worry anyway. At least I would. Not only about Lisa or about how the music had changed or first-gig jitters or any of those things. I couldn't have explained it, not even to Ron, the biggest worrier I know. I just had this feeling that whatever happened next might be the kind of thing that forces you to feel things you've promised yourself not to feel. And makes you say things you wish you could take back. Things were changing too fast. My life felt out of control. Even with all the excitement about finally having a job, it was a sinking, slipping-backward kind of feeling.

CHAPTER 6

*J*ust a Dress

"*B*ut Danny," I pleaded, whispering because Mark and Ron would be joining us any minute. "Patti wouldn't bother anybody at this party. She would just sit at the back of the room and listen."

"Lisa, this is a *private* party," Danny stressed. "You can't go dragging uninvited people to a private party. It isn't professional."

"But having her there will give me confidence."

He raised an eyebrow. "Like you really need more confidence." He put down his clipboard and placed a hand on each of my shoulders. "Lisa, I'm sorry but we just can't take anybody with us to our first gig. It just wouldn't look right."

I gave up. "All right. Never mind."

"But listen, I'm glad we had this moment to talk privately about Saturday. There is one more detail I need you to take care of."

He let go of my shoulders, but he was still looking

intently into my eyes. "I want you to find a dress to wear."

"A dress?" I repeated, caught off guard. "Danny, I don't even *own* a dress."

"I don't mean a fancy dress—simple would be better. Something long, maybe even black. Something to make you look older."

"But I can't—"

"If you're worried about the expense, the band will cover it."

I shook my head. "It's not the expense. It's just that . . . I've never . . . I don't have a clear idea . . . maybe . . . maybe you could come with me, Danny, and help me?"

Danny sighed. "You know I can't do that, Lisa."

"Why not? Why couldn't you? If anybody saw us, couldn't you just tell them it's business?"

"It's not just being seen. I've got a million other things to do to get us ready for this gig."

"I haven't shopped for a dress . . . in years," I said. As I was saying it, a shadowy memory came into my head—myself, younger and wandering through a mall, tripping over my own feet in weariness, someone walking with me, tugging my arm, not listening, rushing me. Mark. Mark telling me I needed a dress. A black dress for the funeral.

Danny interrupted my thoughts. "Couldn't you ask a friend to go shopping with you?" he asked helpfully. "How about the one you can't bring to the party?"

But how could I ask Patti now? I groaned, feeling

trapped. Danny looked up at me from the clipboard on which he was making a list of songs and made a sad face, sorry that he couldn't help. We could hear Ron's noisy muffler in the drive; the others would join us in the studio in a matter of seconds.

"I hate shopping," I said pleadingly, wishing I could explain.

"Trust me, Voice," he said. His tone was gentle but firm. "You need to look older."

The bus route to the mall was endless, past the southern lag of Highway 12, past deserted strip malls, gas stations and abandoned houses—a stretch of highway that would make a person feel depressed anyway, even if she wasn't going to a place she hated, a place she'd sworn three years ago never to set foot in again. My stomach was clenched, alternating butterflies and heaviness, and I felt like the other people on the bus could tell there was something wrong with me—like they could see that I was scared.

I was prepared. I had a shopping plan. Once the bus dropped me off at the mall's entrance, I went straight to the biggest of the four department stores, the one that my mother had liked best. I hurried to the junior dress racks and picked out a dozen in my size—all varieties of black, some with patterns, some with flowers, some solid and some plain. I took them in a great heap to the dressing room and began trying them on mechanically, stretching them over my head quickly, one after another, flinging them off, separating them into a Yes pile and a No pile.

When I had tried on every one, I started in again on my Yes pile, throwing a few more into the No pile, until the Yes pile consisted of one dress. It was the best dress. It was the simplest and the prettiest and it fit the best and it changed me. I saw myself transformed. I looked older, much more adult and somber. I fluffed out my hair and stared at my reflection.

I look so much like Mom, I realized. And I remembered that shopping was the only time Mom and I ever really fought, really disagreed. She always wanted to buy dresses for me and I resisted her every step of the way. Now I was looking at myself, my new self, wearing exactly the kind of dress she would have loved to buy for me.

"You doing all right in there?" the saleswoman called from outside the dressing room. Her voice was bright and false.

"I'm finished," I said, smoothing my hair and unzipping the back of the dress.

"Any luck today?" she asked, like we were girl-friends who could talk about it.

"Yeah," I replied. "As a matter of fact, my luck is changing."

"That's great!" she sang.

I came out in my jeans, paid with the fifty dollars my dad had given me and smiled a big blank smile to match hers.

On the bus riding home, I felt excited about the dress, or perhaps it was partly relief that I had accomplished what I had set out to do. The dress was

folded into a flowered bag on the seat beside me; I
opened the bag and touched the fabric, proud of myself. I knew that Danny would be proud of me too,
for doing what he had asked so quickly. I pictured
myself modeling the dress for him, watching his grin
widen. He would tip his head slightly to one side,
the way he always did when something I'd done had
impressed him. *I did it,* I thought happily. It's amazing what you can overcome when you're in love.

I was doing quarter turns to face each of them,
one at a time, presenting myself, holding out the
sides of the flared skirt. By then, I was feeling self-
conscious—it felt so odd to be wearing a dress in the
studio, the place where we had all worked and
sweated and shared pizza and lounged in our dirty
jeans on the cement floor. Danny was looking just as
thrilled as I'd hoped he'd look; tilting his head,
sending me the thumbs-up sign from behind his
keyboards. Ron seemed astounded. "I can't believe
it's you," he said simply.

My last turn was toward my brother. As a silence
grew around me in the room, I realized that Mark
was upset. I could see it in his jaw and in the way his
eyes kept darting away from me and then back again,
away and back, while his shoulders hunched into his
denim jacket, like he was wishing he could disappear. "What's the matter, Mark?" I asked. I looked
at Danny for help, but Danny lifted his shoulders in
a bewildered shrug.

We all looked at Mark. He clenched his jaw, darted his eyes back and forth and just stood there. Danny was standing up now, hands on his hips, losing patience. "What is your problem, Franklin?" he said.

"Chill, Mark," Ron said. "It's just a dress."

At this remark, Mark turned on his heel, picked up his guitar case in one sweep and bolted from the studio. We listened in shock to the sound of him driving away.

"I don't believe it," Ron said in a hushed voice. "This isn't like Mark at all."

Danny turned to me. "Is this dress issue something you and Mark were fighting about before?" he asked.

"No," I said. "We haven't had a fight since I joined the band."

"Do you know what might be the matter with him?"

I shook my head, clenching my arms across my chest, holding back tears. Because I did know. Danny sighed. "This is not a good time for a breakdown in communication, folks."

Ron scoffed, "No lie."

Danny came out from behind the keyboard and touched my arm, steering me out of the studio. "Go home and talk to Mark," he suggested. "See if you can figure out what's bothering him. I'll talk to him too, a little later. We'll work this out. I'll call you tomorrow."

His voice dropped to a whisper. "The dress is fantastic." He took a chance that Ron wouldn't see and kissed my cheek.

I whispered back, "Thank you."

"So practice is canceled?" Ron asked from behind us.

"Afraid so," Danny replied. "Looks like we're taking a night off. Do you want Ron to drive you home, Lisa?"

I shook my head. I would take my bike. The ride might prepare me for whatever would happen between me and my brother. I had a sense of dread about it. My mind was spinning from the way he had looked at me, like the sight of me was hurting him, like it might blind him if he looked too hard.

I put my shawl into my backpack and hiked the dress's full skirt up under me so that it wouldn't catch in the chain. Then I pedaled home. Slowly. Putting off the confrontation. I was going to the place where Mark and I weren't bandmates anymore, just brother and sister, with walls between us and no way to tear them down.

Mark was sitting behind the wheel of his car, playing the radio at full blast, when I walked past him, wheeling my bike to the garage. He got out of the car, slammed the car door and followed me into the garage. "So you're gonna let Danny tell you how to dress now?" he demanded. It made me want to punch him, but I calmly knelt to lock my bike without even looking at him. "You hate dresses," he reminded me. "You've always hated dresses."

He was hovering over me. I stood up and turned and faced him. "Look, this is what I'm wearing Saturday," I announced. "If you have a problem with it, get over it."

"Since when is this band about how you look?"

"Since when does anybody around here *care* how I look?"

"Who paid for it?"

"Give me a break, Mark. Who do you think?"

"Did he pay for it?"

"No, he didn't pay for it! It's my damn birthday present from Dad, okay?"

I stormed into the house and he was right behind me. I was losing it, hating him for how he was talking to me. I knew he was upset, but he was being deliberately cruel. How could he not know what Saturday meant to me? It made something go stone cold inside me. It made me want to be just as cruel to him.

"What is it about this dress that bothers you most, Mark?"

"You don't wear dresses," he said again, but his expression was fearful now.

"Is it because I look so much like Mom? Is that your problem, Mark? That I look too much like Mom?"

Mark's face fell. He didn't look angry and accusing anymore, he looked like he wanted to get away from me. He actually took a few staggering steps backward; then a brief knock sounded at the back door. It was Ron—he pushed open the door and stood in the doorway. "How's my timing?" he asked sheepishly. It was obvious that Mark and I were fighting.

We didn't answer.

"Should I come back later?"

"Don't leave," I said, my voice falsely sweet. "Come on in, we were just talking about who I look like in my new dress."

"Shut up, Lisa," Mark said.

I spun in Ron's direction. "So, Ron. Do I remind you of anyone special in this dress?"

Ron looked trapped. "This is a setup, right?" he asked Mark. "Like no matter what I say, you'll punch me out or something?"

"Shut up, Ron," Mark said.

Ron threw up his hands. "Hey, what is wrong with you two? What—are you both totally stressed out about our gig? Because I personally don't think this is helping."

"I am *not* stressed out," Mark insisted.

"Mark never gets stressed out," I added darkly.

"Well then, allow me to break up this happy family moment," Ron said. "I actually came over here because Danny wants to talk to Mark. He wants us to clear the air right away so that we can have a decent practice tomorrow night. Which I think is a pretty good idea, considering that we lost valuable time tonight."

"What about me?" I asked.

Ron acted like he hadn't heard me. He said to Mark, "He's waiting for you at the Kirby. I can drive you over there now if you want."

Mark nodded, turned on his heel and disappeared through the back door. "What about me, Ron?" I asked again.

"Danny wants to talk to Mark alone," Ron explained uneasily.

"Won't you be there?" I asked him.

Ron shrugged, even more uncomfortable. "Look, Lisa. It's just that . . . seeing as how you and Mark are pretty mad at each other right now and everything, we thought we could do a better job of calming him down. Danny knows how to talk to Mark, Lisa. They're a lot alike, Danny and Mark."

"They aren't alike."

"They're both control freaks. I should know. I've been putting up with it longer than you have."

"You don't put up with what I put up with," I said.

"I put up with all kinds of stuff, Lisa," Ron said. "I put up with always being in the background with those two. And now that you'll be singing for us in that dress, I'll be even further in the background, if you know what I mean."

I did know. I wanted to say something about how much he contributed to the band, but he cut me off.

"Look, I don't care," he said abruptly. "It's worth being in the background to feel like I'm part of something. Something I helped put together. This band is all I have, Lisa."

"It's all I have too," I reminded him.

"But it's different for you," he said. He scratched his head, nervous because he was complimenting me like this, but he didn't look away. "You can sing, Lisa. Like for real. Not fantasy."

I smiled. But I repeated, "Ron, this band is all I have too."

Mark was leaning on the horn for Ron to come out. Ron backed away from me, anxious to leave. "I gotta go," he pleaded.

I nodded. "I won't screw this up for you guys," I told him. "Tell Mark I'm sorry if I upset him."

"I will," he promised. He seemed relieved to hear me say it.

Mark honked again; Ron turned to leave.

"You guys just wait and see how good I'll be on Saturday," I called from the doorway. "I won't let you down. Tell Mark. I'll prove myself, you'll see."

"I know, Lisa," Ron called back. He waved nervously, scurried down the stairs, dove behind the wheel of his car and drove away, taking my brother to Danny.

Mark-man

"All I'm trying to say is that you can't let this big-brother thing screw up Lisa's first performance," Danny said. We were all three talking with our heads together in the noisy, smoky Kirby Grill. It felt good to be talking about the band, just the three of us—it was making me calm down. Danny kept insisting that he wasn't mad. He was just concerned. "We have to have a smooth performance on Saturday," he said. "All the work we've done so far depends on it."

"I don't know what got into me at practice," I said. I was embarrassed to have lost it like that in front of them. There was no way to explain it. No way to describe my need to just get out of that studio. To get away from Lisa and the way it made me feel to see her in that dress. How much it had freaked me out. That feeling like I couldn't get away, couldn't move, couldn't even breathe.

"I thought a dress would help her image," Danny explained. "Maybe it was out of line."

"I don't think so," Ron said. "I thought she looked about ten years older, I really did. It was *spooky*. And you have to admit, Mark, sometimes Lisa looks too young to be singing the kinds of songs she sings."

"So the solution is to dress her up like some kind of night-club singer?" I asked. But when I said it, Danny and Ron rolled their eyes, like I was doing it again, the big-brother thing.

"Look, why don't you just come out and say what it is you're worried about," Danny said. "Are you afraid that guys will come on to Lisa after our gigs? Is that what you're worried about?"

I glared at Ron.

"No way!" he exclaimed, shaking his head. "I didn't tell him!"

"Ron didn't have to tell me," Danny said. "I've been thinking about it myself, wondering if it's going to be a problem."

"She's not the party type," I said. "She doesn't have any experience. I guess I'm thinking that she won't know how to handle all the attention."

Danny thought about this, nodding. "Would it make you feel better if we had some sort of an agreement to take Lisa home right after the performance is over? At least for the first few gigs?"

"I don't think she would agree to that," I warned.

"If it was Danny's idea she would," Ron pointed out. "Remember? She does whatever Danny tells her to do."

I didn't like hearing that, but I knew it was true.

"I'm pretty sure that I can suggest it in a way that she would agree with," Danny said. "Right on the spot, so that it doesn't look like something we planned."

Ron and I agreed. We were both feeling pretty relieved—nobody was mad, nobody was ragging on me for how I'd screwed up an important practice. I wouldn't have wanted to talk about it, not even with the guys being so understanding. I had decided to just drop it with Lisa too—I didn't want to give her any ammunition to use against me during future arguments. She holds on to things, she remembers things, things it's better to forget. She brings up old garbage at moments when you're not prepared. Like throwing it right in my face how she looks like Mom.

And she remembers that time I took her to the mall, I know she does. That awful time right after the accident when I was supposed to help her find a dress for the funeral. And how she kept saying she wouldn't wear one and how I finally gave in and told her she didn't have to. I explained it to all our aunts and to Gram and told them to stop putting pressure on her and that she didn't have to wear a dress to the funeral if she didn't want to. I protected her, like Mom asked me to.

"Lisa said to tell you," Ron said, breaking into my thoughts, "that she's really sorry that she upset you."

"She told you that?"

"She did, honest. Not sarcastic either—completely serious."

"There you go," Danny said, like this wrapped up everything. "But before we drop this subject, let me just ask you both: Is there anything else we need to talk about before Saturday? Anything else you want to bring up while we have this chance to clear the air?"

I flashed Ron a warning look: Don't complain about the music! But it wasn't necessary; he was sending me the same look. We both knew it wasn't the right time. There was too much at stake. None of us wanted any more conflict. Not with our first gig days away.

"Then let's have a toast to Crawl Space," Danny said. He lifted his glass, knocked it hard against ours. "New beginnings, guys."

It didn't feel like a beginning to me. I think of beginnings as being hopeful, but I wasn't feeling particularly hopeful. Calmed down and relieved, but not hopeful. Everything was too complicated, too unresolved.

We were all still friends, though, and that meant a lot to me. I felt lucky to have friends like Danny and Ron. So I made a toast to friendship and I lifted my glass to that instead.

*P*roof

"*D*on't forget to slow down at the end of 'Runaway,'" Danny whispered to me. "Just like we did it last night."

We were together in the front of the van, driving north along Harbor Drive to the cottage, the sun setting to our left. My heart was pounding so hard, I thought it must be rocking the van. Mark and Ron were holding the equipment steady in the back and I was listening hungrily to every word of last-minute advice Danny was giving me. "Remember after 'Runaway' to start 'Back to You' with that little a cappella introduction—count to four out loud and then just wail into it. We'll be right there behind you, backing you up."

"Okay," I said. My voice was quavering like a child's.

"Don't be nervous, Lisa," Danny said. "If you

screw up on a lyric, just smile that pretty smile of yours and keep rolling. Go right into the next song."

"Right into the next song," I echoed.

I stole a heartfelt look at him and whispered, "Oh my God, Danny, it's happening!"

He touched my hand. "I know."

Then the night you've been waiting for comes and suddenly your dream isn't a dream anymore, it's a reality. It's all around you, like something you always knew would happen. I walked into that beautiful cottage in slow motion, hearing the noise and laughter of the party as if from very far away. I felt both afraid and completely calm. Danny was my rock, giving us all last-minute instructions, going over the list of songs, sending me signals with his hands and eyes, reminding me that he had faith in me.

I belong here, I told myself, and it felt true. *Everything I want to happen will happen now.*

I looked people in the eye, I smiled a real smile and said hello to strangers. I introduced the band, my voice calm and proud, and as Mark and Danny started tuning up behind me, I heard my own voice easing out of the center of me and I knew, with those first few notes, that my singing was going to be perfect. I felt connected to what was happening—I felt pulled and held by everybody in that room. And sure enough, everybody stopped talking and laughing and eating and kissing and they listened to me.

They saw me and they heard me. They listened to my voice.

I sang for an hour—it seemed to pass in a flash. When the last note had been sung, I thanked the audience and the four of us went out to a corner of the deck to collect ourselves. We thought we'd be alone, but a crowd of people came out to join us, to congratulate us and ask us if we wanted anything to eat or drink. By then I was flying—smiling, shaking hands, letting guys I didn't know hug my shoulders and bring me food. I kept catching people's eyes— people were staring at me, curious and admiring. Danny lingered close.

"Don't talk," he said, pressing my arm. I looked up at him; I could see in his eyes how excited he was for me. "Save your voice for the second set. This is going really well."

He pointed to Mark and Ron a few yards away; they both looked overwhelmed by the reception we were getting; they were surrounded by well-wishers, people asking them questions about their instruments, about this or that song. *Who's the girl with the voice?* we heard somebody ask. Danny grinned into my eyes.

The second set began and I never faltered. My voice grew huskier as it grew more controlled. We even started to have fun with the audience because we knew we had them in the palms of our hands; we were teasing each other between songs and Ron was cracking jokes, jokes that had never seemed particularly funny before. The last few songs we did were the best—two sad ballads that I sang completely alone, without harmonies and with only Mark accompanying me on guitar. When it was over, I said good night at the microphone and took a little bow while the audience clapped and hooted and whistled —it was unbelievable. Then everybody was coming over to me and congratulating me and asking me questions about where in the world I had learned to sing like that. People were telling me which songs they'd liked best and about other singers I reminded them of. I kept saying thank you and glancing around for Danny, waiting for a chance to politely break away.

Then I saw them—all three of them back out on the deck, surrounded by people. "Here she is," Danny said warmly as I walked up to them. He touched me lightly on the arm and guided me into the center. "People are taking our business cards like crazy," he whispered to me. "If we'd passed the hat in here tonight, we'd be rich! You did it, Lisa."

"I don't know how to act now that it's over," I confessed. "Everyone is being so friendly."

"I think you should disappear," Danny said.

"Disappear? You mean leave?"

He nodded. "Go home and savor your victory. Trust me. It will create even more of a buzz about you. Besides, you look exhausted. And I need to work this crowd, talk up the band, drum up some more jobs while people are interested. It's better if I do that alone. Ron and Mark have already agreed to drive you home."

Ron appeared at my elbow, Mark behind him. "Danny thinks it's good for my image if I just disappear," I told them.

They both nodded.

"Is the van ready?" Danny asked.

"All loaded up," Ron replied. "We'll take Lisa home and unload it in the morning."

"Slip away, Lisa," Danny said, gently pushing me toward Ron. "While everyone is wondering who you are." He waved at me, backing away.

I looked at Ron. "At your service," he said. So the three of us left with people calling out good-byes and thanking us, telling us they couldn't wait to hear us again. It felt strange to leave like that, with the energy still swirling, but Danny had seemed so sure that it was best. Mark got into the back of the van; I climbed into the front with Ron, who was driving. "Will you and Mark come back to the party later?" I asked him.

"To tell you the truth," Ron admitted, "I am absolutely whipped. What about you, Mark?"

Mark had been silent. He hadn't congratulated me or said anything about my performance. I turned to look at him; he was staring out the window, his expression unreadable. Ron started to ask him again, but Mark interrupted the question. "I'm not going back," he said quietly. "I'm tired too."

"But if neither of you goes back, how will Danny get home?" I asked.

Mark and Ron both chuckled, like this was an extremely foolish question. I pretended to laugh with them, hiding my bewilderment. My head was buzzing suddenly with a deep weariness, a coming-down kind of weariness that made all thoughts spin and blur until I could imagine nothing but my bed-room, my bed and the waiting pool of sleep.

I'll see Danny tomorrow, I remember thinking, wandering into the silent house ahead of Mark, veering into my room, tumbling in my slip into my bed, hugging myself, congratulating myself. *Savor your victory,* Danny had said. I heard his words in my ear as I fell into blissful sleep.

Mark-man

"It went great, didn't it?" Ron asked. It was late morning; we were unloading the van, carrying the amps and drums and mikes back into Danny's garage. The studio was locked; there was an unfamiliar car parked outside the garage and a note taped to the studio door that said, *Wake me up when you want to unload.*

"It went great," I echoed. My ears were still ringing and I hadn't slept at all.

"I wonder if Danny got us any more gigs."

"I wouldn't doubt it. That crowd was totally with us."

"With Lisa, you mean," Ron said. A pause. "She was amazing, wasn't she? I mean, really, completely amazing. Wasn't she, Mark-man?"

"She was."

Another pause, then Ron asked bluntly, "Then why isn't either one of us overwhelmed with happiness about it?"

"Shut up," I whispered. "He's right upstairs."

"I don't think he's exactly listening," Ron said. "Admit it, Mark-man—you aren't completely overwhelmed with happiness either, are you? Are you? God, we didn't even want to stay at the party! We didn't even want to go back and meet girls."

"I was tired," I said. "We played for almost three hours."

Ron raised his eyebrows like he knew better. "We weren't that tired."

I put the amp I'd been carrying down with a grunt and glared across the top of it. "Ron, why don't you just tell me whatever it is you want to tell me and quit trying to put words in my mouth about last night."

Ron's voice fell to a whisper. "Did we become the Lisa Franklin Quartet last night or *what*?"

"I don't know," I grumbled. "Maybe we did."

"But nobody ever asked if that was okay!"

I didn't answer; I was leaning against the amp and thinking about how sometimes old Ron hits the nail right on the head.

"Is that a totally lousy thing for me to say?" he asked. "After how good Lisa sang and how much everybody was digging it?"

"I don't know."

"Is it bothering you too? Because you definitely don't seem overwhelmed with happiness, Mark-man, you definitely don't."

I wasn't. But it wasn't just the confusion I felt about the gig. I was also feeling torn up inside about something my dad had told me just a few hours before. Which I was not about to bring up with Ron. And there was something else bothering me, something else I couldn't have explained. Even though I had agreed to let Danny handle getting rid of Lisa after the gig, it had really bothered me that she had just left like that because Danny told her to. I mean, she didn't even question it; he could have told her to stop breathing and I bet she would have stopped. I don't know why, but it didn't seem good, that she trusted him that much. It just didn't seem like Lisa, who used to ask me a million questions a day and needed everything explained ten different ways and still wouldn't buy any of it.

As if on cue, we heard the sounds of somebody coming down the back stairs from Danny's apartment, and Ron and I shot each other warning glances: Be cool. But when the garage door opened, it wasn't Danny who came out, it was a girl, a tall blond I recognized—the girl who had thrown the party last night, except that she had struck me as good-looking at the party and in Danny's garage she looked wasted. She smiled at us, embarrassed. "Danny's still sleeping," she said. "We got in kinda late."

"You're Kerry, right?" Ron asked her. "The one whose party it was?"

She giggled, nodding, then gushed, "You guys were so fantastic! All my friends loved you, especially your singer—what was her name again?"

"Lisa," Ron said. He looked at me. I looked at him. There was an awkward silence because neither of us could think of anything else to say to Danny's latest. "Gotta run," she said finally. She took a few steps, tripped over a loose wire, dropped her purse, picked it up and hurried away.

"How does he do it?" Ron wondered.

"Let's get out of here," I said. I'd had enough surprises for one morning.

CHAPTER 8

*M*orning After

I slept until noon, until I heard a soft knocking on my door. My dad put his head inside and asked, "Were you planning to sleep all day?"

It was so unusual for him to wake me up that I sat upright and rubbed my eyes awake, wondering why. "Did Mark tell you about last night?" I asked.

"He told me I should let you sleep in. Something about you having a pretty big night last night."

I nodded, sleepy but proud. "It was my first real performance with the band, Daddy," I told him. "Did Mark tell you how great it went?"

"He didn't say too much about anything," Dad admitted. "He seemed to be in a pretty big hurry to get somewhere else."

"It was a huge party," I said, following him out to the kitchen in my bathrobe. "Hundreds of people . . . well, not quite hundreds, but *lots* . . . and everybody listening and clapping and telling us how great we were."

"Mark said he had to hurry up and unload some equipment with Roy."

"Ron," I corrected.

"Ron, right. Anyway, he said I should just let you sleep. But now that you're up I have something to tell you. If you're awake, that is. Are you a fully functioning human being yet?"

My dad isn't the teasing type. I checked out the smile he was wearing and noticed that it was a different smile for him. You could almost have called it immature. Silly. He was trying to joke around with me. I couldn't remember the last time he had done that. I noticed several other things, too. His hair was different—someone had cut it and layered the front, which made him look younger and healthier, even with the thin patches at his temples. He looked less burdened and closed and weighted down. *Daddy is happy*, I realized.

"I'm functioning," I said. "What do you want to tell me?"

He took a deep breath. Pursed his lips. Closed his eyes and stammered, "I'm . . . I'm . . . I'm seeing someone, Lisa."

Big news flash, I thought.

"It's . . . it's actually someone you've met. From the office. Elaine Mitchell, remember her? She's a wonderful woman. Really a fine person. I've actually been seeing her . . . on and off . . . since . . .

well, since January, but I didn't want to say anything to you kids until I was sure."

"Sure of what?" I asked.

"Sure that it will . . . continue."

"Does this mean that this Elaine person might
actually come over *here* once in a while?" I asked
dryly.

Daddy didn't catch the sarcasm. "I was actually
suggesting to Mark this morning that maybe we
could all go out for dinner somewhere," he said.
"The four of us."

The four of us, I thought. *Daddy, give me a break.*
"You said all this to Mark?" I asked.

Daddy nodded, but admitted, "Mark acted some-
what more surprised than you. I had kind of hoped
we would all sit down and talk about the . . . pos-
sibilities, but he rushed off."

Big surprise. "Mark doesn't like discussing pos-
sibilities, Daddy," I said. "He prefers cold, hard
facts."

"Well, I don't have any cold, hard facts about
this," Daddy said. "It's all very new for me. I just
felt that it was time to make an announcement. And
so I have."

He leaned back in his chair, looking relieved and
pleased with himself. I felt a core of annoyance growing, annoyance at how completely he had replaced
my announcement with his own. And his was six
months overdue. A fact which would not have been
lost on Mark.

"What were you planning to do today?" he asked.

"Nothing," I said. "I'm kind of tired from last night."

"I guess I'd better tell your brother to bring you home a little earlier next time," he said in his best fatherly tones. "You need plenty of sleep at your age. Your brother should keep in mind that you're only fifteen."

I didn't even bother to correct him. I said quietly, "You do that, Daddy. You tell Mark not to forget that I'm fifteen. That will be a big help."

I got up to leave the room. "What are you doing today?" he asked again.

"Staying in my room," I told him. "I have important things to do in my room."

I stayed there until I heard him leave the house, driving away to his precious Elaine.

$\mathcal{D}$anny met me on the run at the water's edge, hugged me and lifted me up and hugged me again. It felt so wonderful finally to be with someone who understood what last night had meant to me. "You did it, Lisa," he kept saying. "It was all you!"

We sat down in the sand and went over the performance song by song together; he made a few suggestions, but mostly, he praised me. Kissed me and held me and praised me. "What did you do all day?" he asked. "How did you celebrate?"

"I waited for this moment," I confessed. "But this afternoon, I was writing a poem about my dad and I started hearing a melody in my head as I was writing it. It was the clearest, surest melody, Danny. And I said to myself: This must be what it feels like to write songs! Maybe I could show it to you?"

Danny kissed the top of my head. "Sure, when things settle down, Lisa. Right now we have to stick with getting prepared for the next gig. We have two more confirmed party jobs already next week—one of them for Wednesday night, the other for next Saturday. Didn't I tell you this would happen? Crawl Space is *rolling*! And these two gigs will get us even more gigs, and it will build and build until by September we'll be fighting them off, Lisa. Fighting them off."

He hugged me as he spoke, rocking back and forth with excitement. We were giggling like children who have pulled off an amazing prank. But then he drew back and held me at arm's length and asked, "Did you talk to your brother today?"

"He was already gone when I woke up. My dad said he went to your house to unload the van. Didn't you see him?"

Danny shook his head. "I got up really late and the van was already unloaded. I thought it was kind of strange, though, that they didn't come up to talk to me about how great things went last night. Especially Mark."

"I think my dad told him something this morning that might have bothered him," I explained. "Dad finally got around to admitting that he has a girl-friend."

Danny looked puzzled. "So what? Why would that

bother Mark? My dad has a different girlfriend every week. Big deal."

"It's not like that for us," I said. "My dad hasn't even gone out with anybody since Mom died. I wasn't surprised, but I'm sure Mark was. It's a big change. And Mark doesn't like surprises."

"That's why Mark can't ever find out about you and me," he said.

"He won't," I promised. "No one knows—I haven't told a soul. Mark doesn't suspect a thing. He still thinks I'm twelve years old."

"No, he doesn't, Lisa," Danny said.

I didn't want to talk about Mark anymore. "Tell me about the new jobs, Danny. Do you think I should do the same songs I did last night?"

"Exactly. And I also think we should keep everyone guessing about who you are."

"You mean—"

"Disappear right after your performance again, just like last night."

"I don't always want to disappear, Danny!" I said. "I want to promote the band too. And meet people and be a part of things."

"There'll be plenty of time for that later in the summer," Danny said. "Right now, it's important to build your reputation. Trust me. It worked like a charm last night. There was such a buzz about you in that room. People kept asking me—'Who was she?' 'Who's the girl with the voice?' " He hugged me again.

"When will we practice?" I asked.

"Our gigs will be our practices now," Danny explained. "Playing at parties two or three times a week, making contacts the rest of the time."

"Then we can meet alone like this more often?" I suggested hopefully.

But Danny looked troubled. "I'm not sure," he said. "Things are actually going to be even more hectic for me than before. For the sake of the band, we may have to hold off. I know you can appreciate what an important time this is for moving the band forward."

I nodded, crestfallen but determined not to show it. I wanted Danny to believe that I could handle whatever was best for the band. His arm around my shoulder was both firm and gentle. "You're so different from other girls," he said into my ear. "You understand how important the band is to me. I love you for that, Lisa."

He had said it! He had said he loved me! I sat beside him, letting him kiss me, feeling both wildly happy because he'd said he loved me and filled with sadness because he'd also said he didn't think we could see each other more often. He was asking me to believe in his love, but not to need to be alone with him. I put my head on his shoulder and smiled up into his eyes, acting strong, even as I wondered where I'd find the strength.

So there were two more jobs like the first one that next week, two more parties on the north side, gatherings of older kids, some who had heard me at the first party. The jobs started out with the same swirl of nervous energy, the heart-pounding ride to the party in the van, the buildup of welcoming vibes as we set up, the circling of curious people forming around us, waiting for us to begin. Danny sent me glances, private smiles, winks of encouragement. Sometimes we would exchange a press of fingers, a leaning into each other, shoulders touching. Then I released my feelings into songs.

The response grew. Danny had predicted that interest would build, and it was happening. By the third party, people were actually requesting songs, applauding most loudly for their favorites, calling out my name when the set was over.

But there was another pattern building, at Danny's insistence—the expectation that I would disappear after each performance. More and more, I would hurry out to the van with a sinking feeling— a feeling that it wasn't necessary to leave like that. That it wasn't fair.

So I had to live with a new strangeness—each time we played there was the incredible high of the performance, followed by the letdown of being pulled away, sent home. Sometimes when I left the parties I would see Danny talking to some girl, someone who couldn't possibly know that he was mine, and it would make me want to run back inside, run into his arms and tell everyone to stay away. But of course, I could never do that.

And something else had changed. By the last week

in July, we weren't rehearsing at all anymore. I went
back to an earlier pattern of being in the house alone
on the nights when we weren't performing. I felt
even more cut off from people on those nights, after
all the intense togetherness of practices. We had all
been so united then, me and the guys—so hopeful
and determined—like a family. Once we started performing, it was like we were all scattered again, not
talking, not meeting, coming together only at dizzy-
ing parties for two or three intense hours of performing, a swirl of people, a time of exposing my heart in
song after song, an exchange of congratulations,
an ache in my chest because I couldn't publicly
be with Danny, and a feeling of being wrenched
away.

The rides home with Mark and Ron were a weary
tunnel of silence, all the excitement fading away.
"Do you ever miss practices?" I asked Ron once,
driving home, Mark silent in the back.

Then I felt guilty for sounding ungrateful. But to
my surprise, Ron agreed. "Yeah, sure. All the time.
Like how we would just sit around up in Danny's
apartment, talking about the songs we liked and
how we were gonna rock this town. Show everybody
that we weren't losers, no way."

Then I realized that he was talking about the
times before I came into the band. "I meant practices
with the four of us," I said, a little hurt.

But Ron was still smiling his sad, lopsided smile.
"Oh yeah," he said, almost in a whisper. "I miss
those times, I really do."

Mark-man

Ron was always begging me to say something to Danny. "You're the one he listens to. He won't listen to me."

"He won't listen to me either," I told him. "He'll just accuse me of doing the big-brother thing again."

"No, no, this isn't big-brother stuff anymore, Mark-man. This is about music. This isn't *personal*. You have to talk to him, this is totally screwing me up, including my playing—you heard how bad I was last night. Everybody heard. I'll be a joke in this town pretty soon!"

"Quit pressuring me!" I told him. "I didn't ask for this mess. I'm the one who didn't want her in the band in the first place, remember? You and Danny talked me into it, remember?"

This would shut him up for a while. But when I was by myself, I would go over in my head the right way to bring it up with Danny—the right words to tell him that there was a problem. I didn't know how I was going to be able to explain it in a way that would make sense. When it was going so strong, when we were getting jobs, when we had started actually making money. It was like I could hear myself saying it, sounding like an idiot: *She's too good, we're too successful, it doesn't feel right, Ron says it's affecting his playing . . .*

Suddenly I had to avoid everybody in my life, everybody from before. There was nobody I could be around who wasn't bugging me, not even Ron. There was no safe place, not the house, not the studio, not Danny's, not Ron's—everywhere I went, somebody was asking me to fix something or explain something or tell somebody what they should do.

I started going down this path from our house, down to the beach, and just sitting there, at the water's edge, sitting by myself. It cleared my mind, it helped me. I don't know how many times I would walk down there—sometimes twice a day. I felt strange about it, like maybe I was turning into one of those guys who's always lurking at the beach, trying to pick up girls.

I definitely wasn't trying to pick up girls at the beach. But I was sure thinking about one. That one. The one who watches me. Twice now, she's come to the parties, standing in the back, looking at me like I'm the one she wants to get to know, a blond girl with big, black-circled eyes. Knowing eyes. Wise. Or like she's seen a lot. She stares at me, like she wants to ask me something. And she looks like somebody I could really talk to, somebody sensible and pretty, somebody I wouldn't have to avoid. When I glance up from playing my guitar, she's looking me right in the eye and she doesn't look away. But when the set is over, she's always gone.

I don't even know her name.

Once when I came up from the beach, thinking about her, I saw Dad fixing a broken railing on the deck. He stopped hammering and looked at me as I came up the drive. "Just thought I'd make a few repairs," he said, like he did stuff like that all the time. When in fact I hadn't seen him pick up a hammer in about ten years. His face was kind of twitching as he said it; maybe he could read my mind. I know I make him nervous, now that I know all the facts about his secret life. "Whatever, Dad," I said.

"Say, Mark, have you seen your sister today?"

"She's in her room."

"No, she isn't. I just checked."

"Then I don't know where she is."

Dad tapped the hammer on the railing beside him, getting ready to say something, taking his time.

"It's really hot out here," I said because I wanted to get away.

"Listen, Mark. Lately I feel like you and your sister are avoiding me."

Don't take it personally, I told him silently. *I learned it from you.*

"It's just that we've been so busy with our band," I said out loud. "We have all these commitments like every single day. It's a ton of work."

But Dad was shaking his head, not completely accepting my explanation. "Look, I know I'm partly responsible for how we've drifted apart as a family. I mean, let's face it, I haven't exactly been the most involved parent—"

"Never mind, Dad," I interrupted. I wasn't about to stand there sweating buckets while he went into ancient history.

"No, let me say this, Mark. I have to say this. Because I want things to change. I want us to change. I feel like I've been given a new chance at life. A new chance at taking part in life. And I really want you kids to meet Elaine. I really do. I'm hoping that—"

"Could we talk about this later?" I interrupted.

It was the last thing I wanted in my life—a get-together with him and the woman he'd been running around with all year when he was supposed to be working late. Leaving me to worry about Lisa, just like he always had. "I'm actually supposed to be running some errands for the band," I explained. "I'm already a little behind schedule. Seriously, I have to split, okay?"

Another lie. I didn't have any errands to run for the band; Danny was basically taking care of every detail. The only thing Ron and I did besides show up to play was load and unload the van and fix any equipment that got knocked around. But that didn't mean I wanted to hang around on the deck, listening to my dad talk about his new chance at a happy life. So I hurried to my car and drove away, pretending to be in a big hurry to get somewhere, giving my dad a manly wave from the bottom of the hill. *Catch you later, big guy.*

As I was driving, nowhere particular to go, I remembered something Ron had said to me the night before. Lisa had sung about fifty different songs, none of which were the kind of song Ron and I liked. "This sucks," Ron whispered. "Markman, it's like we're living a musical lie."

I decided the place I needed to go was Danny's. He was the one I needed to talk to. He was the one I shouldn't avoid. Danny held the key.

His back door was wide open; somebody was up there. I thought at first it might be Ron—which would have been okay —the three of us talking it out, like the old days. But then I heard a girl's voice, pitched high, kind of frantic, asking him a stream of questions: "Who else? Who else did you have up here?"

Then Danny's voice, asking back: "Did I say I wouldn't? Did I ever once tell you that?" I heard the girl's voice rise and crack and break, and then the girl, whoever she was, broke down into tears.

It unglued me, it creeped me out—I can't stand it when girls cry. I've had too much of that in my life. Lisa. I had a flash of Lisa, a kid again, crying herself to sleep in her room and me not knowing what to do, whether to go in or stay out, not knowing what to say that would help. *Don't miss her anymore. Be like me. Don't care.* I stood there like a jerk, cringing on Danny's stairs, overwhelmed with that trapped feeling, when up above me, the girl shouted, "If it's just a game, you should have told me!"

"I never promised anybody anything!" Danny yelled back. "You want to cancel the gig, then? Is that what you want?"

Tonight's gig, I thought. I wondered if it would be canceled. I didn't want it to be. I wanted to see the girl from the last party, the one who watches me. Maybe find out her name this time, find out why she looks at me like that. Like she has something important to tell me.

"Don't blow it, Danny," I whispered from the bottom of the stairs.

But even as I whispered it, I figured there was nothing to worry about. I knew the way Danny operated. He would get the girl to change her mind, whoever she was. He would get her to do whatever he wanted. He knew how to get girls to do things for him. I used to admire that about him. Until back in June, when I'd first started thinking: *What if it was Lisa?*

Now I just take it for a fact. The way Danny is. Lately, though, it seems to me that it isn't such a great way to go through life, leaving a trail of girls crying behind you every time you go anywhere. I sure couldn't handle it. All those tears.

CHAPTER 9

What I Should Have Known

*I*t happened on the first Saturday night in August, the hottest night of the summer so far. Both of our sets were long and strained and we were dying in the heat—Ron's playing had never been worse. My dress stuck to my back and legs, and my hair was like a mop against my shoulders. I was so relieved when we were finished; for once I didn't mind that I was leaving the party early.

Ron seemed to want to leave too. "Let's just get the hell out of here," he said.

"Five minutes," I requested. Because I needed to say good-bye to Danny. Because something was bothering him, I could tell. I was afraid that something had come between us, something I didn't understand.

I found them in the kitchen, leaning against the sink, sipping a beer—Danny and a beautiful girl with curly red hair who had been crying. I didn't know who she was, but Danny obviously did; he was standing with one arm around her white shoulders. When I came into the room, Danny took his arm from her shoulder and straightened up. "L-Lisa!" he stammered. "Lisa, hi. This is Sabrina, she lives here, this was her party tonight."

There was a warning tone in his voice. Sabrina averted her face, like she didn't want me to see her.

"I was just thanking her," Danny explained nervously, "for letting us play."

"I was just saying he's welcome," Sabrina said, her voice thick. She wasn't looking at either of us.

"I just wanted to say good night," I said in a stunned voice.

"Good night," Sabrina said. Dismissing me.

I lurched away, upset, and hurried down the stairs and through the clusters of people at the party. I heard Danny call my name once, but I didn't look back. Then he was behind me, at my shoulder. "Lisa, Lisa, wait up—that was nothing."

I faced him. "That wasn't nothing. What was she crying about if it was nothing?"

"How should I know why she was crying?"

"Was she crying because you told her about us?"

Danny looked at me strangely, as though the question was ridiculous. "Lisa, nobody knows about us," he said quietly. "Look, I can't talk about this now, it's too awkward. Why don't you just go home and—"

"Go home and what? Wait for you to call me? When will we talk about this, Danny? At the next gig you arrange? The next party?"

Danny lowered his head, shifting his eyes around, acting cornered. "Lisa, you're overreacting. Sabrina paid us a hundred dollars tonight, I have to be nice to her."

From the driveway, Ron honked for me. Danny shrugged, like there was nothing more to say. I whirled away without another word, left him where he stood, free to comfort the girl upstairs who was crying for a reason he wasn't telling me.

When I climbed into the passenger side of the van, I stumbled against the door because I was so upset.

"Take it easy," Ron said. "Tonight was bad enough without you breaking your leg."

"Where's Mark?" I asked, noticing it was just the two of us in the van.

"Mark got lucky," Ron said, envy in his voice. "When I left he was introducing himself to some girl named Molly who followed us here from the last party."

Another surprise, but I was too numb to react. I added softly, "I think Danny got lucky too."

"Danny doesn't *get* lucky," Ron grumbled. "Danny lives in a state of perpetual luckiness." He sighed. "Maybe someday it will rub off on us, hey, Lisa?"

I was silent for a long time, letting what he was telling me sink in. Letting it filter through a kind of veil of denial I'd been hiding behind, something about Danny that I hadn't wanted to see or hear. Something I had, in some ways, already known. *A state of perpetual luckiness.*

Ron was silent too, driving slowly through a soft, steamy fog. "You don't have to take me home early anymore, Ron," I told him. "From now on, you can stay and have fun and meet girls and promote the band. We'll stay as late as you want."

But Ron sighed. "I'm too embarrassed to stay, the way I've been playing," he said. "Tonight was a musical nightmare."

"It's only because it's so hot," I said. "The whole band was off tonight, not just you."

But he shook his head. "You were still great, Lisa. I don't know how you do it."

"It'll go better next time."

"Next time," he sighed. "Next time. Sometimes I wish you weren't so nice, Lisa." Then he bit his lip and looked away.

At the water's edge, I heard Danny coming, heard his footsteps in the sand as he approached me. I was hunching over my knees, close enough to the warm waves to let the water occasionally touch my toes. Trying to be soothed by this. I didn't look up at Danny. He lowered himself beside me, but didn't touch me. "You know you shouldn't have left a message on my answering machine, Lisa," he scolded.

"Poor Danny," I said. "Did your new girlfriend hear it?"

"Mark and I came back from the party together, Lisa. What if he had been with me when I played it?"

I said bitterly, "I'm sure you would have come up with an excuse, you always do."

Danny didn't answer. He began picking up little handfuls of sand and gravel, shaking them in a closed fist and then throwing them into the water, a harsh motion. "Sometimes," he said from between his teeth. "Sometimes I feel like nobody really understands how much effort I put into keeping *everybody* in this band *happy*."

I stayed his arm with mine. "Danny, I don't want to hear that. I want to hear about that girl who was crying. I need to know exactly what she means to you."

He stopped throwing sand, but wouldn't speak. And from this I knew that everything had changed.

So I asked him the question that I believed would tell me everything. "Have you slept with her?"

"Oh, God," Danny groaned. "Lisa, don't ask me that."

"Have you slept with her?"

"Don't, Lisa." He tried to pull me close, to comfort me, but I pulled away, disgusted, and he yanked me back, more roughly. I stiffened, resisting him, but he hugged me anyway, a bullying hug. My face was pressed against the buttons on his shirt and I felt an anger coming from within him, something I'd never felt before, anger and confusion, like he couldn't decide what he wanted from me, now that I knew. When he loosened his arms, I pulled away again and this time he let me go.

"I've been so stupid," I said.

Danny threw another handful of sand into the glassy water. "You aren't stupid, Lisa. But you shouldn't have asked."

Then I asked him a second, even more desperate question. "Why didn't you ever want to sleep with me?"

A long pause. Danny covered his face with his long hands and sighed deeply. "Because you're Mark's sister," he said. "And Mark is my friend."

The words cut through me. But when I spoke, my voice was so calm that it surprised me. "Do you want to hear something pathetic, Danny? Something really pathetic? All this time I thought the reason you never wanted to sleep with me was because you didn't want to take advantage of me."

Danny uncovered his face and looked at me. "You were right," he said. "But it wasn't just because of Mark. I always said you seemed different from other girls and I meant it. You wanted the same thing I wanted. Bad enough to work at it, just like one of us guys."

"One of the guys," I repeated scornfully, mocking myself. "One of the guys with a girl's voice. The best thing that ever happened to your band, right? And so easy to train. So trusting. Going home early, night after night, like a good girl, never suspecting."

"Why are you talking this way? Nothing has changed between us, Lisa."

"Oh, I think something has changed," I corrected him.

"Then *you* changed it," he said.

"Whatever." Despite the heat, I was shivering. "I'm tired," I told him. "I'm sure you are too. I'm going up to the house." I stood up and pulled my shawl tight around my shoulders.

Danny grabbed a corner of my shawl and tugged it, holding me there. "Don't tell Mark, Lisa," he said.

"I won't tell Mark," I said, without looking at him. "No one will know. And I don't want you to worry about how this will affect my singing. I'll sing better than ever, you can count on it."

I needed to get away from him quickly. I knew that I was leaving the secret meeting place for good, that there would be no more secret meetings for us. But I would have died before I'd let him know how much it hurt me. No one would know that either.

The next day, in the late morning, I wandered down the driveway and walked the mile and a half to Patti's house for the first time that summer. She came to the front door with a baby in her arms and a toddler hanging on one leg. Both sisters were whining and tugging; Patti looked completely bedraggled. Then amazed to see me. Then bedraggled again. She squared her shoulders and lifted her chin. "Well, well," she said coldly. "The Voice herself. Such an *honor*."

I couldn't blame her for being angry. I had promised to call her weeks ago. "Are you busy?"

"Obviously. I'm baby-sitting—the story of my
life. Sorry it's not as exciting as the story of yours."

But she opened the door and I followed her into
the house, through rooms cluttered with toys and
baby clothes. The kitchen was a mess—dishes piled
at the sink, used pots and pans in stacks on the stove.
Someone had spilled a cup of juice on the kitchen
floor. While Patti slipped the baby into a high chair
and lifted her other sister into a booster, I wiped up
the spill. She finished making peanut butter and
jelly sandwiches. We did this in silence, unsure how
to begin talking to each other. Once the kids had
quieted down over their sandwiches, I broke the silence. "I'm sorry I haven't called," I said. "We've
been—"

"Let me guess," Patti interrupted. "Really, really
busy?"

I nodded guiltily. "Crawl Space actually started
performing a few weeks ago."

"So I heard."

"You heard?"

"Sure, I have my contacts in the outside world. I
ask around. I request details. You'd be surprised
what I know."

Her tone was unsettling. "Maybe you should tell
me what you know," I said.

Patti made a put-upon face. "Hmmmm. Let's see.
In a nutshell? New band around town, so-so, musi-

cians passable, halfway decent lead guitarist, bass
player and drummer—forget it."

I started to protest and she held up a hand. "Let
me finish. There's this fantastic girl singer. Everybody is wondering who she is. Very mysterious.
Never sticks around. No one can figure out where
she came from. Imagine the surprise when I tell
them it's my best friend of long ago, Lisa Franklin."

I lowered my head, flinching.

"Oh, and you'll appreciate this part," Patti went
on. "Apparently after the rest of the band leaves,
Danny Fabiano goes around bragging to people
about how he discovered you *and* taught you how to
sing."

I was starting to cry. Patti had never seen me cry
before; she seemed to realize all at once how much
she was hurting me. "Don't cry, Lisa," she begged.
"I'm sorry, don't cry."

But I couldn't stop the tears.

"I'm just so jealous," Patti wailed. She was suddenly crying too. "I'm having the worst summer of
my life! I haven't had a date in two months and I'm
bored to death and all I do is baby-sit. You get to be
in a band *and* you're getting famous and you never
ever call me. You said we would go to some parties
together!"

"I wanted you to come to some parties with me,
but Danny said—"

"Danny said, Danny said!" Patti accused tearfully.
"Don't you ever get to decide anything in that band?

Especially since every single person I've asked says you're the only good thing about it!"

I wiped my eyes with the backs of my hands. "Do they really say that, Patti?" I asked.

She nodded.

"Well, you don't have to be jealous of me anymore," I said. "It's not going so great, if you want to know the truth. Being in this band is a lot more complicated than I ever thought it would be."

I broke down again. The kids had started to wail, inspired by us. It made us both laugh through our tears. Patti quickly made another sandwich, gave a half to each of them and patted their backs until they calmed down.

"See what I have to put up with all day?" she asked, wiping their noses with paper napkins. She sighed. "Tell me more about how it isn't so great, Lisa. Convince me."

There was so much I wanted to tell her. "It's just really hard working with . . . those guys."

"Especially when one of them is your brother, right?" she said, like she could well imagine.

I nodded. "My brother who still thinks I'm twelve years old."

"And the other one is a Mister Know-it-all who takes all the credit for *your* singing."

"And lies to me," I added bitterly.

"Lies to you?" Pattie repeated, puzzled. "How does he lie to you?"

I hesitated. "Danny is just basically not a very

honest person. And he expects me to accept everything in exchange for the honor of being in his
band."

Patti made a sympathetic face. "That doesn't
sound fair, Lisa."

"It isn't."

"So Mark and Danny—zero for two. What's the
story on the drummer?"

"I like Ron. He's a decent person." I said. "But I
don't think he's enjoying being in this band anymore. His playing gets worse every week."

"Zero for three," Patti concluded. "Are you getting *anything* out of this band?"

I closed my eyes, fighting tears again. "When I'm
singing," I told her shakily. "When it's me standing
at the microphone and I'm opening my heart and I
know that people are listening, it's the most incredible feeling, Patti. It's like finally waking up after
you've been asleep for a hundred years. So, yes, there
is still something positive for me in the band. More
than positive. Something that I really need. Do you
understand?"

I wanted her to understand. I wanted to believe
that she could understand at least this much about
my life.

"I don't think I completely understand," she admitted.

"Oh well," I said.

"But I believe you when you say you really need it.
You do seem really different since all this started."

It was something. She held out her arms and we

hugged each other. " 'Course, you've always been different, Lisa," she said. "More intense than other people even before your situation at home changed. I wish I could actually hear you sing sometime instead of just hearing about it."

"Right now I need to forget about singing," I said. "Let's you and me go out somewhere this weekend. Dancing or to a club on Twenty-eighth Street or something. I need a break from those guys, Patti. I want to do something with you."

"I won't be free this weekend," Patti lamented. "Mom took the weekend shift at the hospital and I promised I'd cover for her both nights."

She looked ready to cry again with disappointment.

"How about if I just come over here and help you baby-sit?"

"Why would you want to?" She made a face.

"I want to because you're my friend." I wanted to be a better friend to her. She already had made me feel less alone. And she had said something that I really needed to think more about. A question I needed to face. *Don't you ever get to decide anything in that band?*

Wasn't it time I did?

Mark-man

"A violin?" Danny repeated, frowning across the studio at my sister.

She had called us together for what she described as an

emergency band meeting, which had really confused Danny because, in his opinion, things couldn't be going better. At first, I was afraid that Lisa had figured out what Ron and I were thinking, but I was wrong. Once we were gathered in the studio, Lisa announced in this jittery voice that she wanted to add the violin to our band's sound. *To make us even more unique.*

I was embarrassed for her. It was the old Lisa, getting all emotional about something that nobody else wanted to *hear* about. I'd had to cancel my plans with Molly for this meeting, so I was dealing with this mix of emotions toward Lisa that I especially hate—feeling protective of her, but also like I wished I could strangle her.

Danny was frowning. "Could you just explain to me," he said patiently, "what makes you think our sound isn't unique enough already?"

"Look, I'm good at the violin," Lisa said. "I've been playing it since I was a little kid. Ask Mark."

They all turned to look at me, but I didn't want anybody thinking I'd had anything to do with this idea. "She's good," I agreed cautiously. "But that doesn't mean I think we should—"

Danny interrupted me. "You mean like you'd throw in a few violin . . . riffs . . . on certain songs?" he asked Lisa.

Lisa nodded. "Especially the ballads," she said. "The ballads would sound much more achy and moody with violin in the background."

The expert on achy and moody, I thought. My mind was starting to wander; I was thinking about my phone call to Molly an hour ago, the first time I'd actually called her. How nervous I'd been. Terrified. She had sounded glad that it was me. *Something's come up this afternoon. Can you do something tonight instead?*

I'd love that, she'd said. Not maybe. Not yes. Not okay. *I'd love that.*

"It's a whole different thing, Lisa," Danny was saying. "Playing and singing at the same time."

"I do it all the time," she insisted. "When I'm practicing in my room at home."

Which was true—I hear her playing the violin in her room pretty regularly. And now she was looking at me again, wanting me to back her up. "It's not the same," I said. I went back to thinking about Molly.

Lisa's voice cut through my thoughts, demanding that Ron quit being so quiet, demanding that he tell her honestly what he was thinking. I looked over at him; he'd been staring off into space the whole time, refusing to get involved. "Don't you have an opinion on this?" Lisa asked.

I had a sinking feeling. Ron turned his head slowly, looked at Lisa and said, "You really want my opinion? My opinion is that I think it would suck."

Lisa stared at him with her mouth open, like he had just punched her.

"What did he say?" Danny asked.

Ron's voice got louder. "I said I think it would suck. Geez, our sound is *pathetically* folky already."

"Our sound is *folky*!" Danny exploded. He threw up his hands and looked at me. "What the hell is he talking about?"

Then I felt protective of Ron. "Hey, let him say what he thinks, Fabiano," I insisted. "Lisa asked him for his opinion. Let him give it."

Ron took a deep breath and repeated slowly, "I *meant* what I said. Our sound is way too folky *already!*"

Danny looked at the studio ceiling in disbelief. "This is just wonderful. Would you mind explaining what you mean by 'too folky,' Ron? Since we do about ten different types of songs, none of which are folk songs?"

"Look, if you don't want to hear my opinion," Ron said, "then don't ask me to come to some stupid meeting I didn't want to come to in the first place." He pursed his lips and crossed his arms and hunched back against the wall; he was through talking.

"Why are you all being so negative?" Lisa wailed. "God, lots of rock bands use violins!"

"You think our sound is 'too folky,' Howader?" Danny cried again. "Don't you be handing me something like that and then refuse to explain it! What's the matter with you people? You don't like our *sound* now that we're picking up two or three jobs a week? That's not enough success for you guys?"

"Maybe this isn't such a great time to talk about this," I insisted, keeping my cool.

"Maybe it *is* a good time to talk about it," Lisa said in her trembling voice. "We're all here, aren't we?"

That's the problem, I thought, staring at Danny, trying to communicate my thoughts. Danny took in my glance and then looked over at Ron, trying to figure out what was going on with us. I said again, more forcefully, "This isn't the right time, Danny."

"When is the time?" Danny asked. "Ron?"

"I don't know," Ron said darkly. "But not now."

"Thanks a lot, you guys," Lisa said. She didn't sound upset

anymore, just angry. "Thanks for being so open to my ideas."

She picked up her violin case and her backpack and stormed out of the studio.

"She's gone," Danny announced. He didn't sound angry anymore either, just really, really concerned. "When should we talk about this, you guys?"

With one voice, Ron and I answered, "Now!"

CHAPTER 10

Saving the Band

*O*n the night I had planned to spend at Patti's house, Patti's mother surprised us and came home early from work. She gave Patti the keys to her car and set us free. "Let's go to the Earth and get cappuccinos," Patti begged.

So we drove downtown and parked in a lot a block away from the Earth—the only real hangout in Grand Haven for minors—and while we were walking to the cafe entrance, we saw Danny Fabiano barreling out onto the street, exiting the Kirby Grill. I spotted him first—his unmistakable profile, a flannel shirt, the black sheet of his hair reflecting light from a streetlamp. I came to a dead stop and stalled Patti beside me. "Slow down," I whispered. "It's Danny. I don't want him to see me."

"Why not?" Patti whispered back.

I didn't answer; I was waiting with a pounding heart, to see if he was with Sabrina. But to my relief,

I saw my brother and Ron spill out of the Kirby behind him.

After the relief came a different kind of left-out feeling as I realized that my bandmates were out on the town without me. Danny had thrown an arm around Ron's shoulder and another around Mark's. They walked that way—three in a line—in the opposite direction. I heard Danny laugh with his head thrown back at something Ron had said.

"What's wrong with you?" Patti asked, reading my face. "Are you upset? Lisa! So the guys were at the Kirby—so what? At least they're not still fighting, right? Isn't that better?"

I nodded sadly, watching the threesome stride across the street, around the corner, until they were out of sight. I felt so left out. *If it's this bad when I see him with Ron and Mark,* I thought, *how will I survive seeing him with Sabrina?*

At the Earth, I struggled to put the incident behind me and just be with Patti. She was so thrilled to be out at all, waving to people she knew, finding us the best table, ordering chocolate cappuccinos. The café was in a beautifully restored old building, with gleaming hardwood floors, bleached brick walls, candles on every table. "Don't you just love this place?" Patti sighed. "I feel like I'm in Italy. Man, wouldn't your band kill to play in a place like this sometime?"

"My band?" I repeated softly. "Playing here?" I toyed with the wax at the base of the candle on our table and let the idea more fully enter my brain, noticing how instantly it eased the ache of feeling left out.

"This is a perfect place for live music!" Patti insisted. "Look—there's a spot for a little platform stage."

She pointed to the front of the café, where three tall, cathedral-like windows faced the street. I followed her finger and saw myself standing in the spot where she was pointing, saw the guys behind me, saw the four of us dressed in black, bathed in the streetlamp light that filtered in through the tops of the tall windows.

"Wouldn't the guys love the chance to play in a real club?" Patti went on. "With a *real* audience?"

"Maybe it would be a way for us to start over," I whispered, nodding as I said it, picturing Danny as I told him the news—a real job, a real audience, a concert instead of a party. I imagined the smile that would break across his face, that smile that meant I had gone way beyond his expectations. I heard his voice in my ear: *You saved my band.*

"What are you grinning about?" Patti asked. She reached across the table and gave my arm a teasing punch. "Oh well. It's a nice fantasy, right?"

"Let's find the manager," I said.

Mark-man

Danny came out of his kitchen, rubbing the back of his head and frowning. "That was your sister on the phone," he told me. Ron and I were sprawled on his beat-up sofa with our feet on his coffee table, watching MTV and eating subs from the take-out, just like the old days.

"What does she want?" I groaned.

"She asked me to call another meeting."

Ron groaned too. "Not the violin thing again?"

"No, something else. She wouldn't tell me on the phone, but she said it's good news. I told her you guys were already here so she's coming over. You know anything about this, Mark-man?"

"Negative," I said. "I haven't laid eyes on Lisa all week."

Danny shook his head, puzzled. "Man, she sounded so happy."

That makes two of us, I thought. I'd spent the past two days with Molly, getting closer and closer to her. It felt like the entire direction of my life had changed; I wondered if the guys could tell.

"If Lisa's calling a meeting," Danny said, "we have to all be in agreement that we won't say anything about what we've been discussing the last few days. The way I see it, there is absolutely no point in bringing up any of this new stuff until we're sure."

Ron made a face. "Like we're not sure!"

"We're *not* sure what we're going to do about it," Danny said.

"I don't see how we can sit around at another band meeting," I said, "listening to another one of her crazy ideas, without at least letting her know there's a problem."

Ron agreed. "It's dishonest, isn't it?"

"Hey, don't forget you were talking about *your* little problem with our sound for weeks before you let me in on it," Danny reminded him.

Ron sank back into the cushions guiltily. "That was different. I wanted to be sure I wasn't crazy. With everybody saying how fantastic she was, I thought maybe I *was*."

"You told Mark," Danny said. "You should have told me."

"You wouldn't have listened," I said, and then I was surprised that I'd said it. Danny looked surprised too, but I didn't take it back. "You were too psyched about how everything was working out with all the jobs, Danny."

"Okay, okay." Danny backed down. "So now we're finally in agreement, everything's out in the open, and my point is that there's still no rush to say anything to Lisa."

When I scowled at this, he exclaimed, "It could take months to work this out, Mark-man! What are we supposed to do, turn down jobs and sit around and do nothing for the rest of the year?"

"But Danny," Ron said. "Wouldn't it be kind of like we're using Lisa?"

"No!" he exclaimed. "Look, all I'm saying is that we do this *gradually*. We'll ease her out. It'll be easier for her and better for the band if we don't hurt her."

Ron and I looked at each other. We knew there was no way to do this without hurting Lisa.

"Okay, you two," Danny said. "Maybe you'd rather I told her right now? Just as soon as she gets here, we'll all break the news. You think that's a better idea?"

I told him no way. I'd already made it crystal clear that I was not going to be around when he told her. It wasn't my job—Danny did the hiring and firing. And I was planning to be as far away from her as possible, maybe even out of town with Molly, hiding out. Anything to avoid seeing the look on Lisa's face when she got the news.

"Danny's got a point," Ron said. He was about as eager as I was to be around when Lisa got axed.

"So we're in agreement then?" Danny asked.

I looked at Ron; he shrugged unhappily. We weren't exactly in agreement. But we didn't want to argue with Danny —not with things feeling so much like the old days. So we told Danny that we agreed.

So you can imagine what a shocker it was, sitting around the studio like we were still the happy foursome, having Lisa announce in this thrilled voice that she had gotten us this amazing gig at a wonderful coffeehouse downtown. I'm saying that she had it all arranged—without asking any of us if we were even remotely interested in this kind of gig, which we definitely were not. "You guys aren't mad at me for not asking you first, are you?" she asked—brilliant deduction— because we were all being so quiet. "I just really wanted it to be a surprise."

Danny jumped in smoothly. "We're all very impressed that you did this on your own, aren't we, guys?"

Ron and I grumbled yes.

"The manager promised me that if we pull in a lot of people, we can play there again in September," Lisa said. "I told him we'd print up flyers, get the word out, make sure people know so we'll draw a good crowd."

"You told him we'd print flyers?" Danny repeated. I could tell he was struggling not to lose it.

She nodded. "The manager's name is Mack—he's really, really nice—and he wants you guys to come in and meet him and talk to him about our sound system, tell him if we'll need anything special—"

"Wait a minute, wait a minute, there's something I don't get," Ron interrupted. "You said you gave this guy a tape to listen to? But we don't have a tape."

"I sort of made one," Lisa admitted. "Although I told Mack that it wasn't a real demo since it was only me on the tape. I absolutely stressed that there are four of us. Mack said he wanted to hear something that would give him an idea of the kind of songs we do. So I just sang a few songs into a tape recorder with . . . my . . . violin."

Then her voice kind of trailed off, like she was realizing that the violin part might be the last straw. We were silent, all three of us, completely stunned.

"You guys aren't acting very excited," Lisa said. The understatement of the century. "Look, I promise you I'll take care of everything—I'll do all the work myself for this gig."

Danny was suddenly standing behind her; he made a get-happy gesture, drawing a smile on his face with a finger, trying to get us to act more enthusiastic. But we couldn't. It just couldn't have been more wrong—the idea of us doing a coffeehouse gig now. Lisa promoting Crawl Space with a tape that had only her on it. Lisa turned around, stared at Danny questioningly, like he was going to tell her what to do or say next, like he had the answers.

"Way to go, Lisa," he said to her. He even put his arm around her shoulder. "We're all kind of overwhelmed. Let me drive you home and we'll talk more about it. The guys and I will stop over at the Earth tomorrow and talk with this Mack person. Maybe after that, the whole thing will seem more real."

Danny is smooth, I'll give him that. Lisa smiled with relief and didn't glance back at me or Ron. Danny walked her out of the studio, guiding her by the arm with one hand, giving me and Ron the five-minute sign with the other.

"I feel sick," Ron said when they were gone. "I actually feel sick. It's a plot to make us feel as guilty as possible, that's what it is."

"I told you we should have told her."

"You think Danny's going to want us to go through with this coffeehouse deal?"

"I don't know," I sighed. "We'll find out when he comes back."

"You know how he is," Ron said. "He'll pump her all up about what a great thing she just did for the band. Then he'll come back here and tell us how we have to do this deal . . . one more time . . . for the band. And we'll say yes. For the band. That's the way it works around here, haven't you noticed?"

I nodded, covering my face with my hands. "I don't want to argue about this," I mumbled. "I don't want any more hassles. I just want the band to move on."

I said the same thing that night to Molly. I was telling her how Danny had come back after about an hour and had done exactly what Ron had predicted he would do. And how Ron was saying that he thought it was really dishonest to act like we were still a band when we weren't. "I let them do the arguing, I just kept my mouth shut," I told Molly. "I felt like I didn't know anymore what was the right thing to do. Either way seemed bad. And I just want the band to move on."

Molly was listening carefully. She always listened to me like she believed that if she listened hard enough, she would understand what I was saying and what I wasn't saying—the parts I was leaving out. Then, after listening, she would say something so right, so clear-minded that it always made me want to grab her and kiss her. Which I was doing frequently anyway, for about a hundred other reasons.

"What do you think I should do?" I asked her. She hadn't said anything for a long time.

She'd been looking out over the water at the sunset, but now she turned and faced me, looking me straight in the eye. Half her face was pink from the sunset; the other half was shadows and dark colors. It looked bizarre. But I was thinking all the same how much I liked her face—everything about it.

"I think that if no one told your sister the truth before now," she said, "then you three guys all have an obligation to do the job at the Earth with her. And do a really, really good job —play the best you've ever played. So that everyone there will think she's fantastic and she'll be able to find some other band if she wants to, just like you guys are going to find a new singer. That's what I think, Mark. Does that make sense?"

Molly made everything make sense. I put my arms around her and I thanked her.

"But you have to tell her the truth about what you've decided," she added.

"Right, but I'm not telling her," I said, feeling cornered. "Danny's going to tell her."

"But if Danny won't tell her," she insisted, "then you have to do it."

"Look, you don't understand. There is no way that I—"

"Because you're her brother, Mark. You have to take care of her, she's only sixteen."

Something exploded in me when she said that. I don't

know what else to call it but an explosion. I felt something roaring up inside me and I jumped up and started walking away from her so that I wouldn't yell right in her face. But she jumped up too and came hurrying along behind me. "Mark, you know I'm right," she called. She tugged my arm so that I would turn around.

"You don't know!" I cried, unable to stop myself from shouting over the water. "You don't know what I went through with her. You don't know anything about me! About what it was like for me! Don't be giving me that 'You're her brother' stuff! You don't know what it's like being Lisa's brother!"

"Mark, why are you yelling at me?" Molly asked. She looked completely stunned. It brought me back, made me realize that I'd lost it. And I was stunned too, shocked that I had exploded like that in front of her. I couldn't even look at her. "Was I yelling?" I asked sheepishly.

I thought, *She must think I'm crazy.* I had crossed my arms and was trying to breathe normally. She tugged my arm again so that I would look at her. She looked very calm, not mad at all.

"What got into me?" I asked.

"I don't know exactly," she said. "But you're right about one thing, Mark. I don't know what you went through with your sister. I don't know a lot of things about you, because you haven't told me. I don't even know exactly how your mom died. So why don't you sit back down here with me and tell me and then I'll know."

She was staring up at me. I looked away from her, holding back.

She put her hand on my shoulder, leaning on me so I'd sit back down with her.

But I stayed standing. "I can't," I told her. "I can't talk about it."

"When, then?" she asked. "Mark, you'll have to trust me. When?"

"I don't know. Not right now!"

"Then, *when*? *When*?" She wasn't backing down. "Look, Mark, you know that I'm really serious about you. When are you going to open up to me? When, Mark?"

I told her soon.

CHAPTER 11

Heading Toward Earth

"You are so amazing," Patti said in a hushed voice, watching me brush my hair in my bedroom. "I mean, I can't imagine myself ever getting up in front of an audience and singing. But look at you, the concert is next weekend and you're not even scared!"

"Yes, I am," I said. I confessed something to her that I hadn't told anyone else. "I have this pain in my chest from fear. I have it all the time. Sometimes I think it's never going to go away." I pressed my hands over my heart. "It's like a secret."

"You say the strangest things!" Patti exclaimed. She looked worried about me, so I changed the subject.

"This is what I'll be wearing," I said, taking my dress out of the closet and laying it at the foot of my bed.

"What a great dress!" she exclaimed. "It's so *retro*!

Why don't you wear your black shawl with it—it
would go perfectly." She pointed to where it was
hanging on my bedpost.

I was thrilled that she thought so. I wrapped the
shawl around my shoulders and stood in my jeans in
front of the mirror. "I wanted to wear it before, but
the guys decided it was a little too much."

Patti scoffed at this. "So now you're taking fashion
advice from your band?"

I laughed, pulling the shawl tighter. Patti was
such a good influence, reminding me to decide for
myself what I wanted. "You're coming tomorrow
night, aren't you?" I begged her. "I really need you
to be there."

"Of course I'll be there! Are you kidding? This
will be the highlight of my entire summer. I'm
bringing Amy and Karla and Elle and Tony. They
saw the flyers you put up and they are treating *me*
like *royalty* because I told them that you promised to
dedicate a song to me."

I was so glad to hear this. I needed to know that I
could look out into the crowd and see a true friend.
It had occurred to me that Sabrina might be in the
audience too and that I would have to accept it, and
stay strong and focused and not let her affect my
singing. It would be my hardest test. But if I passed
the test, then maybe Danny would realize that I was
better for him than she was. In his car, driving me
home from the studio, he had praised me, like he
used to. "You're so much like me, Lisa," he'd said.

"You don't wait for other people to do things for you, you go out and make it happen for yourself."

Standing at the mirror, I put my hands over my heart, holding back the ache of hope that these thoughts brought with them. I told Patti again, "I really need to have you in the audience."

"You don't need me," Patti said. She said it proudly. She didn't understand what this night would mean for me. What it would require. Such a terrible strength, such a hardness. In the mirror, she smiled in approval and fanned the shawl at either side of me, making it a cape.

"You look like such a gypsy," she said. "Especially with your hair."

My dad came back later that same day from a business trip—a conference for accountants over in Lansing. He came into the kitchen, carrying a grocery bag filled with apples and pears from a roadside market. I was at the table, eating vegetable soup I had heated from a can. He was wearing a summer sportscoat—off-white linen, another present from Elaine, who was gradually replacing his entire wardrobe. "Hey, kiddo. How was your weekend?" he asked.

"All right. How was yours?"

"Very enlightening," he said. A word I had never heard him use before, so I figured Elaine must have gone with him. "Anything new to report on the home front?" he asked.

"We have a job at a coffeehouse this weekend," I told him. "That new place downtown, the Earth, kind of a hangout for high school kids. It'll be a real turning point for our band."

"Good for you," he said. "How's that brother of yours doing these days?"

"I don't know. He's never here. I think he might finally have a girlfriend."

My dad turned from the counter to look at me in surprise. "A girlfriend? Really? How serious?"

"Daddy," I informed him slowly, "that is *hardly* something Mark would tell me."

"Well, is it anybody I know?"

"How could it be? You don't know any of his friends. Or mine either."

He looked stung. He turned around again, unloading the apples into a wooden bowl—clunk, clunk, clunk. Then he stopped what he was doing, hunched over the counter a moment, then whirled around and blurted, "Sometimes I get the feeling that neither of you wants me to know your friends. That neither of you wants me to know anything about you anymore."

When I didn't deny it, he continued in a rush. "I get the feeling that you'd rather I never asked you what you're doing, never tried to talk to you, never made any plans around you at all."

I didn't deny any of it. I just looked at him. He lowered himself into a chair and sat across from me so that he could look at my face. "Would you like me to meet some of your friends, Lisa?" he asked.

He waited so intently for my answer, his eyes round, his glasses halfway down his nose, new tortoiseshell glasses, expensive-looking. *Elaine*, I thought. I replied quietly, "I only really have one friend, Daddy."

He nodded enthusiastically, like this information was much more success than he'd expected. "Well . . . is one friend all you want?" he asked.

"No. One friend is all I have."

"You have Mark," he pointed out. "You've always had your brother."

"No, I haven't," I said. "Mark changed a long time ago."

He drew back from me, his face rearranging itself. Then he sat forward again and asked, "Are you angry at your brother because he has a girlfriend?"

I said no. Because honestly, it was the last thing in the world I was upset about.

"Are you upset because I have a new girlfriend?"

"No!" I insisted. "I'm glad you have a girlfriend." As I said it, I weighed it to see if it felt true. It did. What difference did it make? "I've noticed that it's making you happier."

"I *am* happier," Daddy said. "I've been so much happier, Lisa—I can't tell you. I'm afraid to believe it. But sometimes when I come home and I try to talk to you and Mark, I get the feeling that I waited too long to get happier. I let the hard times drag on too long. I know I did, I couldn't help it. And now it's too late for some things. Like being around for Mark. Or knowing your friends and having them

know me. Or you and I ever doing anything together. Please tell me the truth, Lisa. Is it just too
late for those things?"

He looked ready to cry. My father was like Mark;
he never cried. I didn't want him to lose it, right
there at the kitchen table; I wasn't prepared. But I
couldn't say no. I couldn't lie and say it wasn't too
late. I just stared back at him, wishing he'd go away.

"Would you like me to come to this place downtown and hear you sing this weekend?" he asked.

It was an alarming idea—Daddy in the audience.
Daddy listening to me sing all those sad love songs,
songs about finding a man and losing a man and
having my heart broken. Daddy, who had never seen
me in that light, who still thought of me as a little
girl. He didn't know me, didn't know what I had
been through that summer. The thought of him in
the audience seemed too sudden and too alien. I
didn't know how to tell him. So I just looked at him.
Maybe he could tell what I was thinking. Finally he
said, "Or would it make you too nervous to have me
there?"

"Kind of," I said pleadingly.

"That's all right," he said. "I wouldn't want to
make you nervous. I'll do something with Elaine and
you can tell me about it afterward, okay?"

"Okay," I said. "I'll be sure to tell you about it." I
couldn't hide my relief.

"Okay," he said again. He couldn't conceal his
disappointment. Maybe he was regretting all those
months of leaving me home alone. Maybe he was

realizing what it had cost. We both quickly left the room.

That same evening, after Mark got in, I knocked on his bedroom door. I needed to talk to him about tomorrow night. I had handled nearly all of the preparation myself, wanting to prove to the guys that I could take responsibility for putting the entire event together. The weekend before, I'd made flyers on Dad's computer and posted them all over town. I'd chosen the list of songs. I'd handled the preparations at the café. The guys were letting me take control of everything. I was glad, but also afraid that I would forget something important since it was my first time.

"Mark, can we talk a minute?" I called through his door. He opened his door but didn't come out of his room. "Do you feel like we're all set for this weekend?" I asked him.

He stuck his head around the door. "Did you tell Dad about me and Molly today?" he asked back.

I was startled. "I—I guess I mentioned that you might have a girlfriend," I stammered. "That's all I said. Her name is Molly?"

"Look, I want what's happening between me and Molly to be really private. I don't want Dad grilling me about my personal life."

"Did you tell him that?"

"Basically. I told him it was no big deal."

"So are you saying it *is* a big deal?"

"Look, I want it to be private," Mark repeated. "I

don't want to have to explain it or discuss it. Understand?"

"Okay," I said. "Her name is Molly?"

He nodded and repeated it, like it was a very intense word for him to say. "Molly."

"Will she be at the Earth Saturday?" I asked.

He looked evasive. "Maybe."

"You could introduce me to her, if you want."

He shrugged, noncommittal.

"Whatever," I said, disappointed. "Listen, I just wanted to ask you if you're happy with the list of songs I picked. Because it's not too late to make changes. Did Danny and Ron seem happy about the list? I thought maybe we could use it for our next few concerts too."

Mark was becoming more and more fidgety, drumming his fingers against the door. He said vaguely, "Maybe you should discuss this with Danny."

"I can never reach him," I said.

"I think he's home now," Mark said. "Call him." Then he shut the door.

Maybe I'll ask him in person, I decided on the way back to my room. *I can always tell him it was Mark's idea.* As soon as I had let this thought enter my mind, I wanted nothing more in the world than the possibility of seeing Danny, just once before the concert, just to talk to him. To be in his apartment again, even if it was only for a few minutes, even if it meant nothing to him—it would mean so much to me. I knew it was backsliding. I didn't care.

But even as I rode my bike over there, and as all the old early-summer feelings for Danny came rushing over me, I knew I was making a big mistake. Sometimes you know you're heading for something that will hurt you, but you keep pedaling and pedaling anyway—you can't stop yourself, you can't do the sensible thing.

From the back stairs, I heard a girl laughing, so I guessed that Sabrina was there. But I went up anyway. I wasn't thinking anymore, I was just moving in a straight line up those stairs, like someone in a dream. At the door I saw them at Danny's kitchen table laughing with their heads close together. The girl saw me first; she stopped laughing and squinted, first at me, then at Danny. I had never seen her before. "Uh-oh," she said. "You must be Sabrina."

"No," I replied. "I'm not Sabrina."

"Whatever," she said. "I was just leaving." She stood up, then exclaimed, "Hey, I recognize you! You're the Voice! The singer, right?"

I looked at Danny. The girl got up from the table and left the apartment, scurrying down the stairs, calling out a teasing good-bye to Danny like it amused her to be leaving him with a girl who was upset with him. Then we were both silent, listening to the sounds of her car driving away.

"That was nothing," Danny said. "She was just here to talk about a job."

I nodded. "Right, a job. Did you take it?"

"No, I don't think we'll be taking any more jobs

until September. I think we all need a break. Once
we get through tomorrow night, we're going to lie
low for a while. Get ready for fall. Understand?" He
sounded frazzled, nervous.

I nodded. "I just came over to talk about last-
minute details for the Earth."

Danny's phone rang. He got up and went into his
bedroom to answer it, a bedroom I had never seen.
Suddenly I wanted to see it—this might be the last
time I would ever be in his apartment. I followed his
voice, heard him say hello to someone. My brother.
Hey, Mark, what's up? He didn't sound nervous anymore. He was turned away from me, facing the wall,
cross-legged on his rumpled bed. Danny's bed—I
took in the sight painfully, my eyes resting on a
small beaded purse at the foot of his bed, something
left behind. "Look, I can't talk about this right
now," Danny was saying into the phone. I paused,
waiting to hear if Danny would tell my brother, his
best friend, that I was there, now that it no longer
meant anything if I was there or not. "No, I'm
alone," Danny insisted. "But I'm expecting somebody any minute about a job."

He lies so easily, I thought. *Were any of the things he
told me true?*

Mark-man

So the day before the Earth gig, Danny suddenly announced
that he's decided it's my job to tell Lisa. I wasn't having any
part of it—I told him flat-out no. The afternoon of the gig, he

brought it up again and I said absolutely no. Loading up the van, he brought it up again, and I exploded. "Hey, I'm the guy who didn't want to have her in the band in the first place, remember?"

Danny put down the amp he was carrying and balled up his hands. I actually thought for a minute that he was going to take a swing at me. But instead he pounded the top of the amp a few times and then leaned over it, covering his face. "Look, I know she was my idea," he groaned. "But I'm telling you straight out—I just can't do this. I can't tell her. I thought I could, but I can't."

"I'm not doing it for you, Fabiano," I said. "I'm the one who's gonna have to live with her after you tell her. I'm the one who'll pay the longest."

I didn't feel sympathetic toward him. I knew that he didn't want any more conflict in his life—he was having major girl trouble, but the way I saw it, he brought it on himself, the way he was always stringing some girl along, always keeping somebody in the wings.

Ron had come back into the garage from the van. "Quit fighting, you guys," he said. "Let's just get through tonight and figure out the rest later."

"We need to do more than get through this," I told both of them. "We need to play our best for Lisa. This is her last night and the least we can do for her is—"

"She's here!" Ron whispered. She came in a few seconds later, wearing her ghostly black dress, and that shawl she loves so much around her shoulders. She had big hoop earrings on and an expression on her face that dared any of us to question what she was wearing. Nobody did. Maybe it was the earrings and the shawl, I don't know, but it suddenly seemed like she had matured about twenty years since the beginning of the summer. I felt a pang of guilt, realizing how much she'd grown up—guilt and disappointment in the band because none of us had found the courage to be straight with her. In a way, we were treating her like a little kid, somebody we could sneak away from. And she still thought we were behind her all the way. She didn't know.

"Shall we go?" Lisa said. She sounded cold. It made me almost wonder if she knew something was up. But that wasn't possible. I looked at Danny. He was looking at Lisa too, probably feeling the same tidal wave of guilt that I was feeling. He sure looked it. But Lisa wasn't looking at either of us. She turned on her heel and left the garage, heading for the van. The three of us followed her.

This is going to be a very strange night, I thought. All the way to the Earth, nobody said one word.

People started trickling in while we were setting up—two and then three and then a few more and a few more, until pretty soon it was a stream of people, filling the tables, needing more chairs, taking their places at the back of the café. "The place is already full," Ron whispered to me. "And they're still coming."

I wondered if this would spook Lisa, but she seemed more calm and controlled than I had ever seen her. Some school friends of hers had netted a ringside table, and Lisa drifted back and forth from the table to the equipment like a human battery getting recharged. Danny's friend Sabrina was on the other side of the room, sending Danny looks that made it perfectly clear that he was the person she most wanted to kill in the universe. I swear, I don't know how he can keep it all together with ex-girlfriends showing up every place he goes. I was nervous enough with Molly in the audience and she was smiling at me like no matter how lousy I played, it would sound brilliant to her. Once or twice I managed to slip over to the table where she was sitting, needing just to be next to her, like it would give me strength. "I just want this night to be over," I whispered to her.

"Do it for your sister," she whispered back.

Then Lisa stood at the mike and wrapped that shawl around her and put her head back and sang into that mike like it was exactly what she'd been waiting her whole life to do. I swear I never heard her sing the way she sang in that packed-to-the-walls café. It was like she was trying to break every heart in the place. But with total control. She had that entire crowd in the palm of her hand. She was amazing.

About halfway through the single long set we did, something completely unexpected happened. I almost couldn't believe my eyes. My dad came wandering into the Earth. He was by himself and he came through the back entrance and stayed in the shadows, where he probably thought we couldn't see him. I actually don't think Lisa did see him; the Earth could have emptied out completely and she wouldn't have noticed; she was in such a trance from her own singing. But I sure saw him. And I felt this rush of anger coming over me, making me fumble at my guitar, making my mind go blank for a few seconds; I had to struggle to stay with the song. *What right do you have to be here?* I asked him silently. *Like all of a sudden you care.*

I almost started to cry. Right there on that stage, I was suddenly struggling not to cry. *Look at Molly*, I coached myself. *You'll be okay if you look at Molly.*

But I couldn't look at Molly. I couldn't take my eyes off Lisa. It was like for a few moments it was just me, my dad and Lisa in that room. And I was feeling so many emotions all at once —anger, guilt, regret, love. And something else—that terrible old feeling of someone missing. I swear, it was all I could do to keep playing. It took all my self-control not to break down in front of the whole damn town.

Finally, after what seemed like ten hours, Lisa announced that the next song would be her last number and that she would sing it a cappella. And she sang one final song about a southbound train she was leaving on tomorrow—a song I remembered from somewhere, although we had never practiced it as a band. *Hold on*, I was telling myself. *Hold on. It's almost over.*

And then it *was* over. Lisa said good night to the audience with everyone clapping and cheering. "Thank you all for coming," she said. "And I want to thank the other members of the Crawl Space—my brother, Mark Franklin, Ron Howader and Danny Fabiano—it's been such an honor to work with these guys throughout the summer. They changed my life."

Behind Lisa, Ron and I looked at each other, both feeling like someone should take us out and shoot us. More applause. I looked toward the back of the room once more, but my dad had disappeared. People I knew and people I didn't know were coming up to the stage and congratulating us. Mack was shaking my hand and asking me when we could come back and play again. Somebody had gotten me a tall glass of cold water and I drank it like a person dying of thirst. Then there was this moment where Danny disappeared with Sabrina and it was just me and Lisa and Ron and the equipment, the crowd finally starting to drift away.

Ron blurted, "You were the greatest tonight, Lisa. You absolutely killed them. You are unbelievable." His voice was trembling—I had never heard him sound so emotional. He put out his arms, like he couldn't stop himself, and he hugged Lisa really hard and she hugged him back in this extremely clumsy embrace. As she looked over his shoulders and caught me watching, feeling so helpless and guilty and proud of her, I saw her eyes filling with tears.

And then she was gone; she disappeared into the crowd with her friends. I turned around, looking for her, and found Molly standing beside me. I groaned and put my arms around her and buried my face in her hair. Molly—the only girl in the room who knew what tonight had really been about for me. The only girl in the world who knew what a coward I was, and she put her arms around me anyway and told me she loved me.

How had I made it through my life this far without her?

CHAPTER 12

The Saddest Song

I had to beg Patti and the other girls to take me home, they were so sure that what I really needed to do was celebrate my night of triumph. Because there was this party and we would all go together and there would be dozens of guys all dying to meet me and on and on and on. "I'm tired," I told them, and they tried to convince me that my energy would come back if I came with them. They didn't understand the kind of tiredness I was feeling, the tiredness of having done the hardest thing you have ever done in your life, having made everything happen by yourself, poured your heart out for hours and then afterward feeling this terrible sense of it being finished. Of falling into such emptiness.

Something is over, I was thinking. *Something is gone. I can't explain it.* All I knew was that I needed to be where it was safe to cry.

"Take me home," I begged them, and so they gave up arguing with me and drove me home.

My dad was waiting there. I came in and found him in the living room, sitting on the couch with his head tipped back against the cushion, like he was planning to fall asleep there. I thought at first he *was* asleep. I had started to tiptoe past him when he lifted his head, and I saw that his eyes were red; he'd been crying. "Daddy, what's wrong?" I asked him.

"Nothing's wrong."

I came closer. "Daddy, something's wrong."

"I canceled my plans with Elaine tonight, Lisa. I came down to that café and listened to you sing."

I couldn't believe it. "You were *there?*"

"I was standing way at the back so that I wouldn't . . . make you nervous." He closed his eyes, overcome, and covered his face.

"Don't cry, Daddy," I begged him, although now I was crying too. "Please don't cry."

"You have such a beautiful voice, Lisa," he said from behind his hands. "Such a beautiful, beautiful voice."

Then he uncovered his face and went on, "It made me remember . . . all the singing. All the singing we did around here. Even I used to sing, remember?"

I had a memory then—how Mom used to call Daddy Johnny-one-note because he couldn't sing at all, couldn't remember lyrics, couldn't carry a tune. But she would make him sing with us anyway, in his droning monotone, rounds and lullabies and car songs, the whole family singing, taking turns, Mom orchestrating. "She kept us singing," I said. "She kept us all doing things together."

My dad lifted one arm for me to sit beside him on the sofa. When I did, he put his arm around me and let me put my wet cheek against his shirt. And because he was letting me cry, I told him a huge, forbidden truth. "I miss her so much," I said.

"I do too," he said. "She did everything for me, Lisa. Everything. Sometimes I think she did too much for us. We never stood a chance without her."

"Will it always be like this?" I asked him. "Feeling like something is missing even when I do something as amazing and important as what I did tonight?"

"I don't know," he said. "I wish I knew the answer. I wish so many things tonight."

"One thing especially," I said.

"One thing especially."

"It's so sad, isn't it? That she wasn't here to hear me sing tonight?"

"It's the saddest song of all, Lisa," Daddy said. "God help us, it's the saddest song of all."

The feeling that something was over stayed with me all week. The concert began to feel like something that had happened years ago, and I let it fade away. My dad, who had been out of my life for years, was suddenly around every evening; I could hear him talking to the computer or taking a shower or watching basketball on TV. I wondered if Elaine missed him.

We never talked about anything; we were just there together, sharing the house and trying to get over that episode of falling apart on the couch. I wanted to tell him that he didn't have to hang out with me so much just because we had cried like that, but something kept me from saying it, so I wasn't quite as alone, and maybe it helped.

One night in a dream, I heard Mom humming in the basement. In the dream, I took my violin from its case and followed the sound of her humming because I wanted to tell her about the concert, about how I had made it all happen myself. I was trying to explain it, but she kept interrupting me to ask me to show her my hands. It was like she didn't want to hear about the concert at all, she just wanted to see my hands. Finally I held them up for her to look at and I saw that they had shrunk—they were too small, like a baby's hands. She said that if I didn't start playing the violin again, my hands would disappear. I tried to tell her that the guys wouldn't let me play the violin, but she wouldn't listen. The dream ended in frustration.

Something is over, I thought when I woke up. *Something is finished.*

Mark-man

"He's already talking to another singer and everything," I told Molly. "The whole thing is turning into some kind of nightmare standoff—like he thinks if it drags on long enough he can force me to be the bad guy."

"He's scared," Molly said.

"He's driving me crazy. And it's not just me. Ron was saying yesterday that he thinks Danny's impossible to work with now."

Molly was thinking hard. "Why won't he just take care of this?" she asked. "Why doesn't he just call her up and tell her? Mark, could there be something personal between Danny and Lisa?"

"No way," I said.

She looked at me and asked it again. "Could something else have gone on between them? Something besides just being in the same band?"

"No way," I repeated. "Absolutely no way. Danny promised me."

"Promised what?"

"Promised me he'd stay away from her. I remember it like yesterday, we were at the Kirby and he looked me right in the eye and he promised."

Molly gave me a torn look, wanting but not wanting to say something.

"Look, Molly," I said. "I know he's not very honest with his girlfriends, but he's honest with me. He's my best friend."

"If he's your best friend then why is he putting you in this position?" she asked.

I sighed. "I don't know."

"Mark, if you don't say something to Lisa soon, she could find out from some stranger that she's not in your band anymore. And after all the work she put into that last concert, think what that would do to her!"

So I admitted something to Molly that I hadn't admitted before. It was like I was admitting it to myself. "Sometimes I worry that once Lisa hears that she's out of the band, something will be over between us. And even though I'm always avoiding her and complaining about her, I don't want to hurt her, Molly."

"It's too late not to hurt her," Molly said. "And you should know that you can hurt people just as much by avoiding them. Think of your dad."

I didn't want to talk about my dad. "Back off me, Molly," I told her. "Just back off. You weren't there at the beginning of the summer, you don't understand."

"I do too understand," Molly argued. "And when this all comes out in the open, it's going to be bad. It's too late to have it come out the right way now."

"Get off my back," I said.

But she wasn't having any of that. "I'm not what's on your back," she said. "If you don't want to talk about it, quit bringing it up."

"God, I feel like everything's falling apart," I said. I felt lost. I reached for her, needing to bury my face in her softly frizzy blond hair, and she let me. She let me wrap my arms too tight around her, even though she was about half my size.

"Not everything is falling apart, Mark," she said.

CHAPTER 13

Zero Without Me

"So how was that job in Fremont last night?" Patti asked me.

"We didn't have a job in Fremont last night," I said. "Danny decided we aren't taking any more jobs until September."

Patti wrinkled her forehead in bewilderment. "Wait a minute—am I going crazy? Amy was saying something yesterday morning about going to hear Crawl Space at a bar in Fremont. Asking me if I wanted to come, but I had to baby-sit."

A pang of something—shock and fear and a strange certainty—went through me, taking my breath away. I reached for a chair in Patti's bedroom and lowered myself into it. "Call Amy," I said. "Ask her about last night."

After a hushed telephone conversation, Patti turned to me and said, "Oh man, I think I might have some very bad news for you."

"They wouldn't take a job and not tell me, would they?" I gasped. But even as I asked it, I was remembering something, realizing something, recalling how during the two weeks since my concert, Mark had been coming home later and later, wearing a familiar smell—cigarette fumes, beer and sweat and something faintly metallic. Hurrying in from his car and heading straight for his room, closing the door before I could ask him anything, just like before the summer.

Patti was still talking; I was hearing her voice from very far away. ". . . some crummy little bar between here and Nunica where once in a while they have live music on weeknights."

"What does it mean?" I asked, interrupting her. "I don't understand—what could it mean if they played somewhere without me?"

Patti asked fretfully, "Do you want to hear the rest?"

"The *rest*? There's more?"

"I guess they had some guy singing with them."

"Some *guy*?"

"Amy said she had no idea who he was. She said he was just terrible. She said that the people she went with all said that the band is a great big zero without you."

"How could they?" I murmured. "How could they do that to me?"

Patti threw up her hands. "Because they're cowards, Lisa!" she exclaimed. "Face it! They're losers *and* cowards!"

"I think I need to go home now," I whispered.

"Lisa, please, please—are you going to flip out about this?" she asked.

"No, I'll be okay," I promised. "I'm not so terribly surprised really. I just . . . I just need to be alone with this news for a while, that's all."

"No, stay here with me," Patti pleaded. "Stay here —we'll make a pizza. We'll take my mom's car. We'll get a video. We'll do whatever you want."

"I just need to go home."

"Will you call me? Will you call me tonight and tell me you're okay? Will you at least do that much, Lisa?"

I heard her voice like she was drifting farther and farther out of my world. I nodded when she offered to drive me home. I honestly don't remember the actual drive. I don't remember saying good-bye to her. I don't remember walking up the steps into the house. I could have walked into anyone's house, ended up in anyone's room. That's how thoroughly I lost those first few hours of knowing what my band had done to me. Of finally realizing what it was that was over.

The doorbell rang, startling me. Three hours had passed since I left Patti's house and I thought it might be her, checking on me. But it wasn't her—it was Ron, standing at my front door, looking scared to death, but also determined.

"I have to talk to you," he said. "Some place private. I have to talk to you in private. Privately.

Alone. Is there someplace we could possibly talk privately alone?"

"Come in, Ron," I said. I walked away from him and he followed me inside, stammering and fumbling with his baseball cap, crumpling it into a wedge, looking so trapped and uncomfortable that I almost felt sorry for him.

"I feel lousy, really lousy," he was saying. "Really lousy. *Incredibly* lousy. Lisa, you are going to hate me for what I am about to tell you. You're going to really, really hate me, but the thing is, I just don't want you to hear this news from somebody who—"

"You're too late," I interrupted. "I already know."

His mouth fell open. "What? What? You know?"

"I know you took a job without telling me and I know you let somebody else sing."

"Damn!" he swore. "Damn, damn, damn—who told you?"

I had wandered out onto the deck, thinking how ironic it was that Ron was the one who had come to tell me. Not Danny. Not my own brother. "Never mind who told me. Just tell me when you decided to replace me."

"Before the Earth gig," Ron admitted, wincing.

Before the Earth! I thought. A knife in my heart.

"We were planning to tell you right after the concert," Ron went on. "Because we didn't want to screw up your performance, see? But then Danny and Mark started fighting about who should tell you. Danny was saying Mark should tell you because he's your brother and Mark was saying Danny should tell you since it was his idea to hire you in the first place. And in the meantime, nobody told you. And then we got this job. And Danny knew this other singer name Jimmy from Muskegon—"

I whirled around in disbelief, startling Ron.

"*Danny* found another singer?"

Ron nodded. "I know it really sucks that he did that, Lisa. But you must have noticed how it wasn't working out anymore. Because we were never meant to be anything but a garage band, playing rock and roll at parties, making a little money, meeting girls. Look, I know this isn't going to sound like much to you right now, but the thing is . . . the thing is . . . you don't need us, Lisa. You don't even belong with us. I mean, who are we really? Three guys in a nowhere town who started a dumb band. That's all we are. But hell, you can really sing. You have this amazing voice. You've got it all. You'll find another band."

"Please go, Ron," I said quietly. "Get off my deck now. Please. I've heard enough."

"Okay, okay, I'm leaving. But are you okay, Lisa? Are you sure you're okay?"

He'd been backing away; he stopped at the edge of the deck and asked once more, pleadingly, "You're okay, right?"

Something snapped inside me. I whirled around and picked up a dead potted plant from the porch railing and threw it in Ron's direction without even realizing what I was doing. It landed at his feet with a crash, shattering into a lump of earth and shards.

"No, I'm not okay!" I screamed at him. "You guys all lied to me and used me and it is *not okay!*"

Ron was terrified. "Right," he said miserably, kicking dirt off his sneakers and backing away. "Guess I don't blame you. Being mad. At us guys. Guess I'll see you around. Bye."

He took the stairs at a run. I sat down beside the shattered pot, covered my face and broke down and howled.

I was sitting on the deck when Mark swung his car up the drive below me. It was dusk; the lake was like glass and the ravines were steamy, but I was encased in an icy, determined rage. I'd been waiting for this moment all through the hours after Ron left, the moment when I would hurt Mark as much as he had hurt me. I would hit him with the truth—the lie I had spun with Danny. I would throw everything in his face, knowing that it would mean the end of his and Danny's friendship. I knew how Mark felt about being lied to. I saw the way he was punishing Dad.

Mark parked his car and sat behind the wheel for a moment without getting out. When he came slowly up the stairs, I saw that he was carrying what looked like a large photograph. Through my anger came a pang of curiosity—could it be the photograph from his room? Where had he been with it?

Mark didn't realize I was watching him. I studied his face—he looked very tired, tired and anxious and older. It occurred to me that Mark was growing

older as Daddy grew younger. The tired old man in
our house was Mark. Maybe it had always been
Mark. When he got to the top of the stairs and saw
me in the deck chair, he stopped short. The worried
expression on his face deepened, but his gaze held
mine.

He's seen Ron, I thought. I could feel his guilty
energy gathering around me, a personal storm cloud,
making the still air heavier, harder to breathe.

He cleared his throat. "Lisa," he said. "Lisa. I
stopped at Ron's house just now. And he said . . .
he said the two of you had a little talk."

"It wasn't so little, Mark," I said softly. "It was
actually rather huge."

Mark took a deep breath and held it a moment.
Then he said, "You probably hate me."

"I hate all of you," I corrected.

"Look, Lisa, the reason I didn't tell you is because
I strongly felt like it was Danny's responsibility to
tell you. I believed—I totally believed—that he
should be the one do it. So I was waiting for him to
do it."

"You were *lying* to me until he did it," I said. I
sounded surprisingly calm.

"Not lying," Mark said. He was shaking his head,
but he sounded cornered. "Not lying—waiting."

"You lied," I whispered. *Are you ready to hear my
lie?*

But then Mark surprised me. He let his weight sag
against the porch railing and he admitted, "I did lie.

It was a lie not to tell you. I knew it was wrong. But I just couldn't face you, Lisa."

"So instead you made a fool out of me?"

Mark's expression changed. He looked suddenly less torn and guilty, more purely miserable. "You're wrong, Lisa. Everybody thinks we're the fools. That's what they were saying about us last night in Fremont. That's what they'll be saying after every gig we do from now on. We'll be known as the Grand Haven band that was stupid enough to get rid of Lisa Franklin."

Mark had quit talking; he was looking away, off into the ravine, still holding the photograph.

"What are you holding?" I asked him, daring him to tell me, since he was being so honest.

He looked down at it, between his hands, as if remembering he had it. "It's that picture of Mom I used to keep in my room," he said. "I was showing it to Molly."

I was astounded. Completely astounded. "Why?" I asked.

"I was . . . I was trying to explain something to her."

"What were you trying to explain?"

"Something about the way I am," he said.

I looked away from him, thoroughly disoriented, my astonishment blocking my anger. *Mark's told someone about Mom,* I thought. Something I hadn't thought was possible. I sat looking down at my lap in the patio chair while he stood apart from me, holding his photograph, neither of us speaking. Slowly the urge to destroy him vaporized in the heat. "Leave me alone," I said finally. "I'm through talking to you."

And for a very, very long time, I was.

*I*t was late, after midnight, but the garage was unlocked. The studio door wasn't locked either so I let myself in, closing the door behind me. I wanted to be alone in the space, so that I could remember more clearly who I had been in it—what sort of person, so trusting and believing and strong in my love for Danny.

It was obvious that the band was practicing again; all the signs were there—the new sheet music, the cigarette butts, pizza boxes, beer cans. I felt an ache of finality, seeing the proof that the studio had come to life without me. But I also felt, standing in the midst of my old world, that I didn't need the studio anymore. I didn't need their world. I was the Voice. I could have music in my life without Danny.

Then I saw the microphone.

It had been given to me, hadn't it? My birthday present, my reward for working so hard, for waiting in the secret place, for believing. The closest thing to a real birthday present anyone had given me since my mother had died. *It's mine,* I thought. *It's mine.*

I held it against me; it was skeletal and steely and it needed a girl's voice to make it come alive again. It needed to come home with me. I couldn't find the case it had come in, so I carried it home in one piece, the cord wrapped around my arm, hurrying through the darkest streets, avoiding the streetlights. Once home, I slipped it into the house, took it into my room and put it at the back of my closet, with my old dolls and my puzzles and my board games and my violin.

It belonged there. When it was time for me to sing again, there it would be, waiting, like an old friend, the only one from the band who hadn't lied to me.

Mark-man

"Look, Jimmy is really pissed off about the mike," Danny complained. "Are you sure you looked every possible place in your house for it?"

I told him yes for the hundredth time. "I'm telling you, it's not there."

"Some burglar probably stole it out of the garage, Danny," Ron said. "If Lisa had taken it, Mark would have found it by now."

Danny glared at him. "Okay, Howader. If it was stolen by some *burglar*, then you won't mind taking a cut in pay to cover it, right? Since you guys will recall that it was one of the most expensive mikes money can buy."

Ron and I grimaced at each other behind Danny's back but neither of us objected. By that point we were willing to pay whatever it would take to get Danny to drop the whole issue of the mike. But for the rest of the practice, Danny kept glancing at me sideways, like he suspected I knew where it was, or like he suspected I knew something. He was always looking at me like that now—like he was expecting me to trip him up or double-cross him, and when it happened he wanted to be ready.

"Does she have it?" Ron asked, driving me home from practice.

I shrugged. "If she does, she'll never tell me."

"Things still pretty tense around your house?" he asked.

"The worst," I told him. "Lisa won't even make eye contact with me. And my dad is around all the time now, expecting me to explain where I've been, giving me this *look* every time I see him like I'm some kind of criminal. I'm not kidding, I am seriously thinking of getting out of there. Moving in with Molly."

"I wish I had somebody to move in with," Ron sighed. "I thought I'd have some money saved up by now. Who knows —maybe next weekend I'll get lucky and find a girl with her own apartment."

Pretty unlikely in the dives we were playing in. We had a job Friday and Saturday at a little bar north of Muskegon on Old 31. A far cry from the Earth. With the kind of gigs we were getting lately, it was a good thing Lisa wasn't with us—it would have been too depressing for her.

"God, I miss her," Ron said. "I mean, I still think her style of singing was all wrong for our band, but I miss the way she always acted so completely thrilled to be around us all the time."

I knew what he meant. Jimmy hardly acted thrilled to be around us. And he and Danny could never agree on the songs we should cover; Jimmy wanted only songs that he could scream.

"Danny's getting worse," Ron said. "It's almost like he

prefers us all fighting. The way he keeps bringing up issues that he knows we won't agree on, have you noticed?"

"I don't know what's the matter with him," I agreed.

Although I did have a theory. I suspected he was punishing himself. I know I still felt guilty about not having had the guts to tell the truth to Lisa. I figured he probably did too.

In August, Molly found a bigger apartment and I made my announcement to Dad that I was moving in with her. He didn't seem surprised or upset to hear it. He even said, "Well, Mark, maybe it will make things easier for all of us."

It threw me to have him act like it was no big deal that I was leaving. I'd been braced for him to put up a fight, or at least act like it was a really drastic decision. I tried to sort out my feelings about it for a while, procrastinating on the actual move, making excuses to Molly when I was with her and making excuses to Dad when I was home.

I put it off for weeks after I'd announced I was leaving; I don't know what my problem was. Maybe I was wishing I could make peace with Lisa before I split. Part of me knew it was too late. Too late to be a family. But you bounce around when you're about to leave home for good. You have regrets. You make a lot of noise in the kitchen. You sleep too much and complain about your sister using the kitchen phone when you want to make an important call. You accuse your dad of picking on you even when he isn't. Because you know it's over. So you stall.

CHAPTER 14

Good Night, Microphone

So the summer came to its bitter, bitter end. The last day of August. It was so terribly hot in my room that I brought up an old fan from the basement and plugged it in beside my bed. It made this odd, rhythmic thumping—a kind of clattery music—and I liked the sound. I craved it. It was a buffer that kept me from hearing too clearly the goings-on outside my room. My brother coming in way after midnight, banging around in the kitchen, looking for food, talking on the kitchen cordless with Molly, arguing with Daddy about nothing. "Since when are you in charge of my schedule?" he'd yell, and then he'd remind Daddy that he was moving out any minute.

I, for one, was counting them.

I was writing again; I wrote constantly. In the morning, in the afternoon, sometimes I'd even wake up in the middle of the night and write. At first I cried while I wrote, and it was like two things coming out of me together—the tears and the words. Then it was just the words. Then I realized I was hearing melodies. I wasn't crying anymore, I wasn't writing blindly, I wasn't writing poetry . . .

I was writing songs.

7 spent the first week of September at Patti's house, helping her baby-sit. I liked being at her house; it distracted me. Sometimes she would say she wished we could spend our last week before school at my house, where it was so much quieter and more relaxing, but I preferred her place with its clutter and noise. Patti was always apologizing because we were stuck with the kids and couldn't go out cruising in her mom's car, her favorite thing to do. "Quit apologizing," I would say. "Just put on a video, I don't care."

"Okay, but if Mom comes home early and I haven't done the dishes, she'll give me that *look* of hers. Like I don't have enough to do with these brats ragging on me every second. Man, I am never having kids, Lisa. No way."

"Let's do the dishes," I suggested. "Your mom is always so tired when she gets home from the hospital."

"I am not her personal servant," Patti complained. But she started unloading the dishwasher anyway and I filled the sink with soapy water for the pots and pans. While we were cleaning up, I told her something my father had announced that morning over breakfast. "He's planning to ask his girlfriend if she wants to get married."

"Wow," Patti said, her eyes round. "Instant stepmom, Lisa."

"My stepmom," I repeated. "Will she actually be my stepmom? If my real mom is dead?"

Patti's eyes widened. She seemed surprised that I had come right out and said my mom was dead. "I think so," she replied.

"I guess I'd better meet her," I sighed. "I hope she doesn't expect me to hang out in the kitchen with her and sing train songs." I laughed softly at my own joke.

"You have the weirdest sense of humor," Patti said, shaking her head.

When Mrs. Spinoza came home, she thanked us over and over for washing the dishes.

"Just don't expect it every night," Patti warned.

She wanted us to head for the Earth, but I made an excuse. I told her I had promised Dad I would be home early. It would be a while yet before I could walk into the Earth, the place where I'd spent the longest night of my life, doing the hardest thing I'd ever done—singing my heart out while I was letting go of all my dreams of ever being with Danny. I couldn't have explained it to Patti—she still referred to it as my victory night.

We would occasionally see one of the flyers I'd posted to advertise the gig, and Patti always pointed it out to me, like it was proof that I was still famous. "When school starts next week," she predicted, "you are going to notice a big difference in the way people treat you."

"That would be nice," I said.

"And don't you *dare* forget about me when you are instantly more popular."

"Like I would ever forget you, Patti," I said.

I thought she was being overly optimistic about the coming school year. Although I certainly had changed. I had learned I had something no one could ever take away from me. But some of the other things I'd learned that summer I wouldn't have wished on my worst enemy. Every time I saw a flyer and remembered how proudly I'd posted them, doing it for my band, for Danny's love, I wanted to die. Some things take longer to get over, I suppose. I should know.

I had another visit from Ron. Brave Ron, the only one who'd had the courage to tell me I'd been screwed over by my own band. He came up to the house on Labor Day Sunday and found me sitting on the deck, working on a song. "You're not gonna throw anything at me, are you?" he asked, only half-kidding.

"Depends on what you say," I said, also only half-kidding.

He chuckled uncertainly and pointed to the papers in my lap. "Were you writing something?"

I shrugged. "Just getting a few thoughts down. I can talk for a minute."

He settled himself on the deck floor across from me, flexing his back against the railing. "So how are you doing, Lisa?" he asked. He looked exhausted and sad.

"Better than last time, I suppose."

A long pause. "Aren't you going to ask me how I'm doing?" he asked.

"I don't care how it's going with the band, Ron, if that's what you mean."

"It's going terrible. Crawl Space is basically falling apart because—"

I covered my ears. "I don't want to hear this."

He held up his hands, surrendering. When I uncovered my ears, he continued. "That isn't why I came over, Lisa. It's just . . . I have this one question I need to ask you. I don't know quite how to ask it. I know I don't even have the *right* to ask it. But I'm going to just come straight out and ask it. Okay? I'm just going to—"

"Would you just ask me, Ron?"

He inhaled and said in a rush, "Was there something private going on between you and Danny while you were in the band?"

I was genuinely taken aback. "Why are you asking me that now?" I asked. And then I realized that I had given Ron his answer. We stared at each other, disoriented, until I looked away.

"Damn," he muttered. "Damn, I knew it—I just had this feeling. Because of how Danny's been slowly self-destructing ever since we replaced you. I just had this feeling that it might have to do with you."

"Mark doesn't know, Ron."

"No kidding!"

"I was going to tell him, but then I didn't. It seems kind of pointless now."

He nodded, accepting this. "I have to admit, Lisa, I'm surprised. Even though I suspected there might be something, I'm still surprised. I guess I assumed you'd see for yourself that Danny and girls . . . you know. That he was trouble."

"Trouble," I repeated sadly. But I confessed, "He got me out, Ron. I was stuck up here in my sad little world and I needed someone from outside to get me out, and then all of a sudden . . . there he was. He's the one who first made me believe in myself."

"Yeah," Ron sighed, "I felt that way too, in the beginning. When Danny first made me believe we could be a band. Maybe Mark still feels that way, I don't know. I'm thinking of quitting the band, Lisa, I really am. It's too much conflict for me now. And you know how I am about conflict."

I nodded, feeling sorry for him, but also detached, like I had been out of the band for years instead of weeks. It was behind me now.

"I also still feel lousy about the way we handled everything . . . with you and the Earth gig and not telling you the truth and all that."

I shrugged. If he was waiting for me to tell him it didn't matter, he'd leave disappointed.

"Not going to forgive us, eh?" he asked.

"Nope."

He sighed again. "Maybe you should at least forgive your brother. None of us wanted to hurt you, Lisa, but Mark had it the worst, the way he sees himself as your Hector Protector brother."

"I don't know, Ron," I said. "Maybe after he moves out, I'll feel like he's my brother again."

We both chuckled at this irony. He left soon after that, late for a practice, taking the stairs with his shoulders hunched; he was frowning, already dreading whatever would happen when he got to the studio.

The next time I saw Ron was the day that Mark had actually chosen to move out. I was reading a magazine in the living room when Mark answered the doorbell. From where I sat I overheard Ron offering the use of his truck, offering to help carry boxes down to the driveway. Mark refused his help, told him gruffly that everything was covered. At the picture window, I watched Ron lumbering back down the stairs. He stopped at the bottom of the stairs, saw me in the window and sent me a dejected wave.

I turned to face Mark. "Why won't you let Ron help you?" I asked. "It would be so much easier to use his truck."

"I've got Danny's van," Mark said shortly. "Besides, Ron's a quitter."

The tone of his voice upset me—it sounded like the old Mark, so contemptuous of weakness, so above it all. I glared at him, thinking, *Haven't you learned anything?*

"Ron's no quitter, Mark," I said.

"Yeah? Well, maybe you don't know what he pulled on the band this week." Then he looked uncomfortable because he had mentioned the band.

But I didn't flinch. "Maybe you don't know some things either," I said. "About your other so-called friend."

"What are you talking about?" Mark demanded.

I was looking him straight in the eye, all the things I knew on the tip of my tongue, giving me strength even as it made my heart beat faster. Maybe it was because Mark was leaving. I felt like part of my good-bye should be to have him at least see that there was an important difference between Danny and Ron.

I think Mark realized that I knew something he didn't know. Something big. He asked again, more anxiously, "What are you talking about?"

"I'm saying that Ron is still your friend. And Danny isn't your friend. And we Franklins have to be more careful about figuring out who our real friends are."

Molly had come into the room carrying a box of Mark's magazines. She gave me a long, silent stare, something approving in it. Mark saw it too. "Aw, she doesn't know what she's talking about," he insisted, pointing at me.

But Molly just looked at him and I just looked at

him, neither of us backing down. Until finally he stepped out onto the deck and yelled down at Ron, who was waiting, leaning against his truck.

"Come on up, Howader!" he hollered. "Help me get these women off my back."

Sometimes I would go out at night into the darkness, down to the edge of the water, and I'd look out over the lake and think about everything that had happened to me. All the lessons I had learned. About myself, about what I wanted from my life, about what I was capable of, about what would always be missing. I knew that it was important to keep going over it carefully so that I wouldn't lose track of myself when school started.

One thought especially haunted me, and I needed to think through what it meant—the realization that if Danny had asked me to sleep with him in June, I would have said yes. I'd been too lonely and too lost to resist someone as real as Danny reaching for me across a blanket in the sand, making me feel important, telling me that I was the one he needed. When I thought about how Danny hadn't asked me to sleep with him because I was Mark's sister, I had to admit that Mark had protected me after all. Mark, who had been left in charge of me. Mark, whom I had told with such certainty that I could take care of myself. He had saved me from Danny after all. And he didn't even know.

*   *   *

I sensed more changes coming. I believed that my time of living beside the lake was ending; Daddy was starting to talk more and more about moving. Or maybe it was because the summer had ended. And because the music had ended. And because Mark was gone now, living with Molly. We were all finally facing how things end.

Face the music, I thought, listening to the waves, watching the sunset. *Feel everything. Don't be afraid to hurt. Face the music.*

Each night, after I'd said good night to my dad, I would close the door to my room and check the back of the closet to make sure the microphone was where it had been the night before and the night before that. I'd part the clothes on hangers and find it waiting, gleaming in the light from an overhead bulb. I'd even say good night to it, like it was alive. *Good night, Microphone.*

Like a friend you are saving for the future, somebody you know will come out into the light when the time is right and the feelings are strong and the voice is ready. Soon.

BLUE DOOR

by Lisa Franklin

Mother, the door on your dreams is blue now.
I visited your old house today,
Blue as my heart when I used to live there,
Blue as the night I swam away.

chorus: Better to see the sky and the water,
           better to feel, to feel everything.
           Look in the eyes of the ones who have
              hurt you,
           better to sing, better to sing.

I came back to ask if you approved
of the ways we've changed
and the ways we've moved.
Now that my father is doing fine,
and my brother has his life and I have mine,
I'm wondering if all this blue is a sign?
All this blue, Mother,
Are you still mine?

(repeat chorus)

Margaret Willey is the author of *The Melinda Zone* and *If Not for You,* as well as the ALA Best Books for Young Adults *Finding David Dolores, The Bigger Book of Lydia,* and *Saving Lenny.* She lives in Grand Haven, Michigan, with her husband and daughter.